HORNS FOR HELL

RAFAEL NICOLÁS

For Archie.

PREFACE

This book contains the following: graphic violence, animal death/mutilation, sexual trauma, non-graphic sexual violence, necrophilia-esque sentiment, torture, body horror, sexual content, self-harm, suicidal sentiment, issues of sexual consent, depictions of war, mental instability, substance abuse, abusive romantic relationships, depictions of apathy/distaste/repulsion at sex.

My beloved spoke and said to me,
    "Arise, my darling,
    my beautiful one, come with me.
  See! The winter is past;
    the rains are over and gone.
  Flowers appear on the earth;
    the season of singing has come,
  the cooing of doves
    is heard in our land.
  The fig tree forms its early fruit;
    the blossoming vines spread their fragrance.
  Arise, come, my darling;
    my beautiful one, come with me."

— SONG OF SONGS 2:10-13 (NIV)

CHAPTER 1

I n a terrible, unknown calm — the following thought:
Rosier had created, in a sense. It's a knowledge that plagued him, though he knew it wasn't entirely true. He had not made anything from nothing, how God does — though he had never witnessed God create this way either — and he was sure his hands' labor had not bore the great fruit of life but, rather, some mockery of it, some disfigured shadow of it, fluttering and disembodied. Disembody. 'That's what I did. I disembodied him. Asmodeus.' He had created something from pieces, which God had not done. The Lord creates from nothing or so it is said. Rosier realized he hadn't been there at the beginning of time, couldn't know if God had, too, created by disembodying whatever had been there before. Had there been nothing before God? Rosier had always believed so, but now he couldn't be certain.

Had there been nothing before God? Or had He woken from primordial sleep to find His hands bloody, the body of another at His feet? Had the Lord taken the body of someone who must've been a friend and disembodied them to make another thing, something lesser than — though you could only know it's lesser than if you knew what came before. Was this life lesser than the life before God's creating hands? If He had disembodied that life, an angel — doe-eyed, youthful thing — couldn't know. 'But God would tell us, wouldn't He?' Maybe He didn't want to leave them longing for what they, the angels, could not return to. That was why God had punished Lucifer, right? Longing.

Cold, Rosier was lying in bed, staring at a gray, stone wall, wondering how many days he had spent here — the answer was merely four, but he couldn't know without any hint of sun or moon light dribbling into his chamber in the caves. He had, of course, stretched his legs at times, climbed off, walked the corridors, intent to show his face so that neither Asmodeus nor Satan would come to believe something was wrong. He didn't want them to think he was sad. He wasn't; in fact, he was feeling quite little, like *he* were made of quite little. Like he would unbutton his skin and tug it apart to reveal great emptiness where blood should be. 'My soul.' His wings must've been attached to his soul — perhaps, they had been his soul — because since the fall, he'd felt this way, missing something, unable to find any of the hundred feathers that had blossomed out at the moment he had — 'No, don't think of that.' He felt himself rise, a little groan spilling past his lips, before he shifted to sit on the balls of his feet, planted two hands on the thin blanket.

"Agh," Rosier said, then said it again. "Agh!" He should pull his hair out, but he opted to grimace instead, screw his eyes shut, think of laying his feet on the ground and walking, walking. 'It's cold.' Lord, it was. Readjusting, he willed himself off the bed, lowering a bare foot onto bare rock — it would not be carpeted for another few thousand years — and staggered to stand, thinking of traveling the halls as he should, allowing other demons to see that the fallen angel Rosier was still among them, that he had not decided to build himself a tower and try to reach God again. No, he was not going to return to Him. 'He will see that I re-created, like a faux god, and He will hurt me.'

Surely, Asmodeus and that recreated body were out stalking the halls. He didn't often leave Rosier to wake up shivering and alone, but Asmodeus had been suffering some intense pain since last night and perhaps wanted to limp it away at dawn. 'Asmodeus...' He pursed his lips.

The fallen angel of fruit headed for his open wooden trunk of clothing, where he had a mere half a dozen tunics, the majority still unadorned. He should weave another, but he'd have to wander and ask if any demons had spare cotton threads, which he hadn't the energy to do. Yet, as he removed his loose robe and yanked a gray tunic over his head, he saw that it was ripped at the collar and tattered at the ends with hem strings dangling. But he hid away the century-old clothing beneath a more modest shawl and, instinctively, reached to pull his long hair through the collar only to feel the feather-tip touches of the obsidian-dark threads that remained of it. He was sure that he'd never become accustomed to this. Hand trailing, he touched his skull; it had cracked when he fell; he could still feel the dried gash.

Slow, he stood back up and balled his nervous hands in his own clothes as he headed for the entrance. Wooden slabs tied together with root met him, then he tugged that makeshift door aside and stepped into where, here, there was carpet, though not so intricate or divinely made as those in Heaven. There was some light, from torch poles, but it was weak, and Rosier wondered how the two demons before him could see as they painted one of the cave walls. Approaching them, but still far enough away they wouldn't notice him, the smaller fallen angel lifted a hand, touched the dried smears of red on the stone. The beginnings of a beast's face stared back at him in almost the color of blood but a bit too bright, maybe the hue of newly-killed, of the first droplets of bleeding.

"I heard from Satan that we ought to expand westward," — the voice didn't come from the painters, and Rosier turned his head down the uncharacteristically lonely hall to see a tall demon scratching at some stripped fur at his neck and speaking to another, whose skin was marred with discolored lines and spirals that Rosier didn't realize must've been purposeful, instead imagining whoever had scarred him was some fallen angel of art, searching for a canvas. At an inquiry, the tall demon replied, "Oh, he was in that garden of his. But he seemed angry about something — Satan."

'Lucifer,' Rosier thought.

"No, Baal wasn't with him, that piece of shit," said the demon to yet another question. "Probably fucking something outside."

Rosier tried not to listen to the rest of his words, instead shifting his attention, beginning to walk again, reeling in some of the cool air of the cave. He put both hands before himself, fiddling with his fingers, bare, cold, and terribly ringless. Many demons were jeweled now — many of the angels of gems and golds had been damned — but the fallen angel of fruit had hesitated. He was still deciding what to do with himself, this new body that was his old body but also not. Just as he brushed his hand on the wall once more, there was the clamor of feet, of chatter, of a stampede of demons all up ahead. 'Oh, there must've been a trial or a fight or—' He didn't finish his thought, quickly apologizing as the tide of demons reached him, some seeing him, their mouths rippling into snickers. Though some did let him through, others extended their arms to shove him back, playful or malicious. Rosier yelped as he stumbled into a demon, stomped onto his foot, and the stranger growled in response, louder than Rosier's apology, then pushed him right into someone else. Getting knocked from one side to another, the fallen angel of fruit continued trying to trudge opposite the infernal sea, hearing a snide comment that one demon shared to another: "He thinks he's still an angel." The reply was: "Bastard in denial."

Bastard — one of Lucifer's words — fatherless or motherless or something of the sort. Rosier didn't know or want to know. 'Maybe that's what I'm in denial about. About Lucifer.'

Finally, he stepped free from the other demons and found himself in a still populated, though not crowded, corridor, and free to take a breath. Maybe Lucifer would help him find something inside of him that wasn't emptiness; was it hopeless to think so? 'Maybe I just miss him.' Maybe he missed holding the angel against him like when Lucifer was a mere infant, and he was just a housemate who loved him dearly. Why had Rosier ever loved Lucifer? He supposed he loved everyone without reason. A part of him still loved God after all that had occurred. He still loved Asmodeus, too.

Past some more corridors, past an archway, then shuffling through a narrow entrance, he came upon sunlight for the first time in weeks, raising a hand and blinking his muddy-golden eyes profusely. Some wind, too, tossed against him, taking his hair at its uneven shoulder-length and dancing with each strand. Before him, there was about a half acre of beauty — flowers, in a disorganized sprawl of colored petals and leaves, tended to by a hundred bustling bees, these new creatures that Lucifer had fostered into being not long after the demons had groomed flowers to life. They were sweet things, fuzzy and striped, and they made little hums as they flew from petal to petal, collecting nectar to create honey how certain angels had in Heaven. Lucifer had created, in a sense. He had made this Earth what it was. And he, the devil, was standing still in this flood of pinks, yellows, and whites, facing away and toward one of the many towering trees embracing each rounded corner of the garden.

Just as Rosier was parting his lips, a bird, small and stocky, dropped onto Lucifer's shoulder, chirped some notes, before the devil let out a soft hum. "Rosier," he called. "It's lovely you're here."

Rosier blinked, a hand still hovering by his brow to shield him from the great star their prison spun around — like an angel dancing for their Father. "It is?"

"Now that there are so many flowers on Earth, I think someone ought to help them bloom into fruits. You could do it, couldn't you?" Lucifer twisted back to him, the bird tilting its beady head. His expression was serene, almost happy, something about it predatory.

5

"I—" Rosier stammered, shifting his weight. "I might be able to." He wanted to say he couldn't create them, just tend to them; 'I'm not God.'

Lucifer took a step, then another, almost like hops, then he was walking toward him with a playful sway. "You don't sound certain." Rosier swallowed. "You look nervous." The fallen angel of fruit, tepidly, lowered his hand and welcomed the blinding afternoon sun. "Are you well?"

"To tell you the truth, I haven't been feeling very good. I've spent a long time in bed."

"Yes. That's another reason I'm happy you're here." The devil's voice smoothed, turned softer.

"You knew?" 'Do you really know everything?'

"Asmodeus is worried; he told me to check on you. I screamed at him, but I did plan to go and visit you. It's the least I could do." He had reached Rosier now and lifted a hand to tuck a stray strand of hair behind an ear. "For how you took care of me, after all."

"Ah, right." Rosier found himself leaning into the touch, his eyelids half-falling. "Thank you. I'm sure I'll be fine." It's not as if he could die, no matter how much he may have felt like a walking corpse. "I hope it's just been days of rest that I needed."

"You haven't been well for years, I'd say." Lucifer's hand trailed down to his shoulder, then down his arm. "Even if I do think it's gotten much worse recently. Did something happen?"

"No. No, I don't think so."

"I noticed that you started acting this way ever since Asmodeus started walking all on his own. Ever since... Asmodeus has come to rely on you a little less. You don't need to feed or clothe him anymore, do you? It's strange that this is upsetting you.'

"I'm not," said Rosier with a troubled tugging together of his brows, "upset."

"Mm." The devil's touch fell down to Rosier's hand to grip it delicately. "Well, I'm still pleased you're here. Like I said, I'd like to have you help me create fruit. You're a duke, so you should start acting like it." The last words were so sharp that Rosier almost flinched. "I really did miss you at the trial today. It was about stealing. You might've enjoyed it."

"I don't think," Rosier murmured, "I could do something like bringing fruits into being. But I could try."

Without a word, the bird on Lucifer's shoulder abruptly hopped off and fluttered her wings and swooped elsewhere, leaving them, leaving Satan behind with a tight smile. "That's all I can ask for." He tugged on his finger, pulled him along toward the flowers. "Come. Let me show you the lilies."

"Did you," Rosier asked warily, "really yell at Asmodeus?"

"Of course I did; he always speaks to me with nothing but disrespect."

'He doesn't believe in you,' Rosier wanted to say, 'how the others do.' But he simply nodded. "I suppose I should also ask how you've been." He squeezed Lucifer's hand back, and it was cold, though warmed by the sun, perfectly shaped.

"I've been very well."

"Is that true?"

Delightfully, Lucifer laughed, tugged at him again much firmer, and Rosier staggered into his body, but he remained there, pressed close to Satan's side, as they approached the patch of white, happily open lilies — these flowers that had fallen from paradise to join the prettiest angel of all. "Look. Aren't they gorgeous?" Rosier said that they were. "Asmodeus almost stepped on them earlier." The two stopped right before the lilies. "What a clumsy beast he is." Before the fallen angel of fruit could speak, Lucifer added, "He's not right for you. I think you should stop looking after him. You made a body for him when you could have left him to rot, so don't let any guilt hold you anymore. He hurt you." Rosier flinched, started wondering if he'd made a grave mistake coming to the devil, but he didn't release his hand. "Let him go."

There were some birds, singing for love, not far from them.

That night, Rosier was preparing for bed — had somehow motivated himself to wash the sheets with an ash-water mixture and dry them over the fireplace — then pulled on his longest, thickest tunic as he sat on the edge of the feather-stuffed mattress. His stomach was full with hearty bone-broth and flower roots that he'd eaten with Lucifer; it had been delicious even without tasting anything like the wonderful vegetables and fruits of Heaven. 'Will I ever see corn again?' It was better not to ask and linger in what he might never have again. 'Never have again.' Well, perhaps he shouldn't think of anything as permanently gone; he would live forever, after all. He would experience everything again, he was sure, he was still hopeful. 'To be young again.' Faintly, he heard the sound of the door. 'I will be young again, one day. I will meet the world again. I'll make friends again one day.'

A grunt sounded, then the thumping of a wooden cane, trekking the ground. Slowly, Rosier turned; slowly, he exhaled. There was a creature there, shutting the door. It, he, was tall, lanky though with strong shoulders. Many parts of him were discolored, held no cohesion like a symphony with instruments each trying to shout louder than the other; some sections of his legs were furred, with an avian foot on his left, whereas some of his arms were scaled, and his hands were clawed. His face belonged to the angel Asmodeus, as did his long, onyx hair. "Asmodeus," Rosier whispered. On the head of his friend, there were two long, dark horns.

Before responding, Asmodeus finished making his way toward their pile of pillows and blankets on the bed, then fell, heftily, onto it near to Rosier. He dropped his canes, unadorned, mere smooth wooden sticks, and he grunted. "I'm sorry to come back to you so late. I was—" He coughed. "I got very distracted."

Rosier blinked, then nodded, smoothing down some of his tunic and lifting his hand to nervously run through his hair only for his fingers to thread the naked air. "Don't apologize. I'm happy you're back now. I was thinking of going out to look for you."

"I'm happy," said Asmodeus, his voice too grave, "that you didn't." Abruptly, it twisted into a lighter, relaxed tone. "And I'm happy to be back to sleep." He rolled both his shoulders as he rose to sit, teasing his thin talons over the buttons of his tunic, beneath an open robe, to tug it apart and expose each discolored patch of skin, including stripes along the left side of his abdomen. "Do you want to check the stitches?" Rosier always did; he inched closer. "Look, they're all fine." With a swift, singular movement, he tore off his robe, then tossed it from them to land over the rock flooring.

Lifting a hand, Rosier grazed only the air before a trail of small, intersecting black lines that split some lighter skin from darker skin. The darker section had come from a four-legged, once-furred mammal, and the lighter side had belonged to a sea reptile. "Oh. I see." He knew it would only itch and burn Asmodeus if he picked at the stitches, so he satisfied with simple examining for now. "I'm happy to hear it." As Asmodeus undressed some more, pulling his tunic over his head then flinging it aside, he exposed himself to be wearing a wrap of cloth at his groin, hiding himself. Rosier murmured, "Should I get your sleeping tunic?"

"Oh, I can just sleep in this. I don't mind it. It's comfortable." Rosier nodded, parted his lips, but Asmodeus spoke once more: "And how are you? I went to Lucifer this morning and told him to invite you out to drink or have a picnic or anything. I thought he might be able to make you feel better." He shifted to support himself on his elbows, lolling his head over to the fallen angel of fruit. "But if I can do anything—" a flicker of hope in his eyes, though timid "—please tell me."

Rosier stared at him, eyes a little wide, his mouth still open a sliver, but he soon reached for their blankets, began tugging them. "I'm alright. I just wanted to lay awhile. I had some things to think about."

Without hesitating, Asmodeus nodded, then chuckled though it didn't have the natural humor it often did. "Thinking about me?"

"Yes," Rosier said, the ends of his lips twitching. "Thinking about you." He delighted, though not incredibly so, at the little surprise that tinted Asmodeus' cheeks in pink. "It's good to know you've been thinking of me too." He, once again, scooted his body, patted the space on the mattress beside him. "We should sleep. I'm very tired. Thank you for talking to Lucifer."

Asmodeus breathed, some relief at its ends, then grunted and crawled closer. "I'm glad you're alright." He was warm; his side pressed against Rosier's as the latter yanked the covers over them. It was always nice to sleep with Asmodeus like this. "There's a trial happening soon that I heard about; I think it's Moloch. Are you going to deal with it?"

Rosier shrugged. "I don't think so... I really shouldn't be a duke, should I?" There was a touch of somberness in his tone. "I don't know how... to punish anyone." He turned to look at him, then smiled as earnestly as he could muster. "Maybe you should be a duke instead, Asmodeus. I think you'd be better at it."

Asmodeus chuckled but didn't reply to that, instead saying, "Alright, for sleeping, do you want to hug me or should I hug you?"

Rosier noticed that his friend smelled strangely. 'Is that alcohol?' "I'd like a hug," he decided, and as he flopped back down, he felt monstrous arms snake around him, pull him even closer. Asmodeus' chest pressed against him, firm and well-made, a chuckle rumbling the bare skin by Rosier's head. Terribly comfortable now — the fallen angel of fruit breathed by the heat of his friend's throat, nuzzling his nose there. The damp scent on him was almost pure sweat, but there was a strong, musky aftertaste.

'You must've been making sin with another demon.' Rosier's heart ached in such a sinking sensation that couldn't be anything but sadness. 'I shouldn't be surprised.' In a brief flash, he remembered laying on his bed in Heaven, staring up at his friend looming over him — Asmodeus, whose gaze was dead. He had asked his friend what was wrong, what he was doing. 'Why are you,' Rosier had asked, 'touching me?' with a plea to stop twisting his tongue like a poison. But in the present, he was turning his face up and Asmodeus was chuckling again. He leaned down, pecking soft, still-angelic lips to Rosier's forehead, over the mussed bangs.

'When you hold me, when you kiss me that gently — it's like that didn't happen. Like that night never occurred, and we never fell, and I can go pick my fruits and tend to them, to slice them for you. But if you smell like that, then I can't help but remember.' He pressed into Asmodeus. 'And now that you no longer need me, you will remember too, won't you?' He wanted to disappear into him, if only to rinse the smell from them both, but his eyes were heavy, and he tripped, like he did from paradise, into a sweet dream of an old house and an old friend.

THE FIRST MEMORY

Dirty; he was so much dirtier than he realized once he — coughing, spewing out hot blood the same color as the fire raining outside — crawled into the small crevice. With one hand, he was attempting to drag along a heavy body against the ground, hearing their garment scrape against the rocks; with his other hand, Rosier was cradling a head, bundled in a torn cloth that had once been a section of the angel of fruit's own clothing. It had been made into a sling, though its knot had undone itself some hours ago — so Rosier had resorted to carrying it, carrying him. His friend. And his other friend, right beside him. He'd tried to carry them both, earlier, except he hadn't gone past a couple steps before falling back over.

But he'd needed to do this, even if Rosier was trembling violently, barely managing to tug Lucifer's body into the narrow passage at the side of the mountain with him. His vision was spotted with spheres of darkness, and the taste of silver was so abundant in his mouth that he was sure jewelry would soon drip past his lips, over his chest, onto the ground. But no such fall occurred. Only the one that had sent his body plunging from the clouds, spinning, broken wings swishing around him, fluttering useless, but he could not remember any more than that. In fact, Rosier wasn't sure that sensation was real either or if he'd tried to fill in the gaps between Heaven and Earth with fantasy.

His breath returned to him slowly, once he'd slumped onto his back and maintained his sight on the ceiling for many minutes, or even hours, feeling the cracked dryness of his mouth and the crisped blood all over his skin. Dirty. His eyes tried to shut for a moment but then couldn't crack open again; even still, he clutched Asmodeus' head to his chest tighter and pulled Lucifer to lay against his side. He didn't have it in him to move any longer, however much his body was twitching. Outside, there were wails, some animal and some angelic ones, and there were thuds — wildfires knocking down the tallest trees, which in turn kicked boulders along hills, rolling along mountains. Each horrible thing beget another. At any moment, this cave could collapse onto them.

Yet, he'd had no choice but to come here; he had nowhere else to hide. He couldn't leave Lucifer where he was — in the tomb that demons had laid their beautiful angel to rest in after days painstakingly crying over him, trying to bless their tears to heal the favorite of God. They dried themselves over him, chose forever thirst and weakness over having to see Lucifer's body burnt and mutilated into pure red muscle and darkened ash. And they had succeeded, watched as their wet grief threaded through to make Lucifer's hair and body shine as it once did. Rejoicing, they'd kissed him. The praise and worship they lavished on him, however, would too begin to dry.

It was impossible to count the days the fallen angel of fruit had spent curled up by the devil, but count the changes he could. Dozens, turning hundreds, of times — Rosier's thousand brothers began not to weep over Lucifer but to hover strangely over. They touched him like an amulet of fortune. When they began to kiss Lucifer's dead face, hands running through every part of his body, Rosier realized what was happening. Horrified, he'd waited to be alone with the rebel angel, then stolen him away in the night, however brightened it was by the fires surrounding them.

Quiet, he snuck from shrub to shrub, trying to hide from the bands of roaming fallen angels, not knowing where to go, unsure if there was any safe place on Earth at all. From behind a fallen trunk, he'd covered his ears and bit down on cries to try and ignore a gang of the fallen violating one, then tearing out his stomach and continuing their torture in a sadistic frenzy. The thought of them finding Lucifer's body, his *corpse*, and himself had filled Rosier's mind with images that made his stomach lurch in deep repulsion. A part of him only grew more miserable to know that he could imagine these outcomes of violence at all. He had once not known much of gore or viscera, but they had become all he knew.

Now Rosier was choking up; his dry tears scorched their way up his throat, nearly as hot as the flamed Earth all about them, and they burned in his very skull. He could not cry. The hurt in him was so great that he could do no more than play dead. To be dead. 'Father,' he prayed. 'Help me. Please.' But only the echo ever responded. Only memories did. 'Of something trying to pierce me and my city come apart.' Opening his eyes, trying to rattle himself free from the feelings of being pried open — Lucifer's empty, half-lidded stare looked back at him. Roped at Rosier's ashen, brittle fingers — there was dark hair. However heavy his pants filling the cave were, there was even louder gasping coming from Rosier's decapitated friend.

A spout of desperate, rapid-beating-heart panic was teasing him, was gnawing at his mind. When God did not respond, Rosier tried to think in His voice. 'I hate you.' He was staring at Asmodeus. 'I deplore you more than anything. Act against me and suffer sevenfold for your sins.' But the sound of the fallen angel's voice bled through. 'You will eat the flesh of your starving self. Ruin will be your name and rot your body.' Hands overcome with tremors, he lifted Asmodeus and brushed his bloodied mouth against the stray hairs over his forehead. 'I hate you.' Only Rosier's voice now. 'Do not ask forgiveness.' Or was it God's? 'I will hate you forever.' Asmodeus. 'Asmodeus.' Asmodeus.

CHAPTER 2

They kissed in the morning — Rosier and Asmodeus. The fallen angel of fruit had leaned over Asmodeus' sleeping grunts, then tapped his lips against the edge of the demon's mouth. Instantly, Asmodeus had stirred, but smiled, wide, before even opening his eyes. When he croaked a morning greeting, Rosier had the urge to kiss him again, so he did, and Asmodeus moved his lips against his, but Rosier drew back, lingered in the hot breath of his closest friend. He kissed Asmodeus often, though he had in Heaven as well — on the cheek, on the back of his hand, the top of his head. Against his mouth — he'd always suppressed that urge. If there was one pleasant thing of living among demons, it's that Rosier felt some less shame when he wanted to kiss Asmodeus's smile, and he enjoyed having his smiling kissed as well. Though it was a change from how things had been between them before, it was a welcome one.

Perhaps he'd been wrong about last night, been wrong to assume things based off a smell that seemed gone by morning.

To eat, the two traveled to one of the kitchens, then ate at an adjacent, wide room with a long wooden table where some demons had meals already prepared or were carrying it over. In

Heaven, all the angels had had homes, each with a kitchen, but here there were only a few, scattered large kitchens that all the demons shared. In some ways, this was better than before, as well — there was always company to eat with, demons who enjoyed cooking always had mouths to feed, and more openly sharing their ingredients prevented over-consumption of their newly limited resources. Of course, the Earth was quite abundant with life, with greens to eat and with creatures to grill, but it would be both inconvenient and disrespectful to decimate the land around them. The devil had built this Earth by bleeding it out from his very wounds; his fury would be insurmountable were he to see any part of his land desecrated by the touch of demons.

Rosier did miss his kitchen at times — he liked the silence — but he could always eat in his room if he wasn't keen to listen to the rowdy laughter and chatter of fallen angels. Today, he saw Baal nearby, joking with a demon, flirting with another one. Asmodeus was at his side, eating mere nuts. He had lost most of his appetite after so long spent living in deep hunger, so he ate only occasionally and only small things. He vomited if he ate too much, and the rest remained in the pit of his belly waiting for him to replace it once he felt significantly heavy. Angels could digest stars, could digest every created thing, could maybe even eat God if they tried, and so could demons who held still the stomachs of angels, but many did not.

Asmodeus, currently, had the stomach of a woolly beast, which was not only large but could do some minor digestion in its demonic second-life. It would last a good amount of years, hopefully. In the meantime, Asmodeus had gotten quite skilled at handling liquids; he sweated it away, salivated it onto his lips, spat it at the ground, and regurgitated it without issue. His last stomach had forced Asmodeus to urinate like an animal, and he had been so furious about it that he cut out his stomach and, crawling in his own blood, tried to stitch a feline's into himself. But, in the present, he was chuckling, eating his couple pecans.

Rosier lifted some rolled leaves into his mouth, crunching

them between his teeth. 'It's better to be out of bed,' he decided, and as if hearing him, Asmodeus smiled in his direction — handsome as always. 'Maybe not good but better.' He touched his clothing — a tunic and one of Asmodeus' robes — as he looked at all the demons in lesser clothing with exposed chests and bellies and groins. He remembered what Lucifer had told him. "Asmodeus—" What Satan had said about them. "I'm going to speak with Lucifer again." At this, Asmodeus let out a relieved sigh; didn't he know that Lucifer didn't like him? "But I'll join you for dinner. Is that okay with you?"

"Of course, of course. I'll look for some cards, and we can play a game tonight." He spoke quick, like he needed to get every word out of his mouth in one breath, sounding almost desperate. 'Does it bother you so much that I haven't been feeling well?' "How does that sound?"

"Nice. It sounds very nice." Rosier, smiling soft, leaned to peck his cheek.

Two or three demons whistled, and one called, "No fucking on the dining table!" but Rosier ignored them, turning away just as Baal twisted over his face.

"Are you looking for Satan?" Baal's head was tilted, his eyes curious and wide; there were great horns at either side of his head, and his arms were burlier than they'd been in Heaven. "He's in his garden." Rosier was still getting used to this new appearance, no matter how many centuries it had been since he changed. "Or, well, he should still be there."

Having just taken his half-finished plate, Rosier nodded and tried smiling again, as he rose to his feet. "Thank you, Baal." As he walked past some demons, heading to clean his dish, he heard a demon joke that Asmodeus should share him, but he ignored this too, even when Asmodeus twirled a meat knife in his hands then stabbed it between the fingers of the taunting demon, grazing enough skin to have him yelp. The demon of lust laughed at his fear — low, cruelly.

It was noon again, the same as before. And finding Lucifer

proved simple. As Baal had said, he was in that meadow, and he called his name softly, then saw the devil turn to him from across several colorful flower beds, his feet over some tulips. "Have you," laughed Lucifer, "come to help with the fruits as I said?"

"I have nothing better to be doing," Rosier replied simply. 'I have few friends here,' he wanted to add.

"Come, then." Lucifer gestured; behind him, sun streamed through the gaps between branches of the heavy forestry, and light speckled onto him in pale freckles. "Sit with me. I have this flower here eager to grow into a fruit. It only needs guidance." He lowered with perfect grace onto his knees over the ground, and as Rosier warily neared, lowering his body much clumsier, Satan laid his hand over the fallen angel of fruit's, their skin tones just a shade or two apart. "It'll be like creation."

"In a sense," Rosier whispered.

A little laugh, then Lucifer echoed the words: "In a sense."

Rosier had already done that, could still feel the hot blood in his hands of creation, of the animals that would become Asmodeus. 'Forgive me,' he remembered saying. 'This body doesn't want you. I'll have to put another one together.' The first mass of flesh — the first attempt at Asmodeus' body — would have to be thrown out and eaten by whoever happened upon it, and Rosier would begin anew, would cut apart new animals. 'Someone forgive me for this.' "I'm sorry, Asmodeus," Rosier had whispered, his heart aching, his body trembling in the darkness of the cave. 'If I cannot ask God for forgiveness anymore, then I can only ask you. I don't have God at all anymore; I only have you.'

And just like then, Rosier made an attempt to no avail — no petals hardened nor nectar turned fruit juice, but Rosier and Satan were creatures of thousands, millions, of years, and they had learned patience. In Heaven, change was slow, and on Earth, there was variety — there were days that were endless, others that were gone in an instant. Lucifer murmured that the creation of fruit would be slow, how the Earth's healing had been slow. Rosier wondered if Heaven had healed from something, too, some kind of catastrophe. As the surrounding forest cooed the melody of life, he could remember the story of angels-turned-stars, but it was so vague in his head that he assumed it was no more than a myth angels had invented in boredom. It was a waste of time to ponder this, he knew; 'it's a waste of time to ponder.' If the stars were truly angels, then they would've woken by now to help, wouldn't they?

After some hours, Lucifer and him surrendered for the day and traveled to a spring for water and to pick some of the flowers. The devil hummed a pretty tune as they did, with the occasional bird flapping over to land atop his head or on his shoulders before singing along with him. With a breeze blowing through his hair and his long, billowy tunic, Satan was beautiful, almost as perfect as he'd been when Rosier would sit with him in their house in Heaven, and he'd been braiding the waves of golden hair as the youthful angel kicked his feet. Before him, the devil offered a wide smile and spoke: "It's been a pleasant day with you. Tomorrow morning, we should try this again." Rosier turned over a pebble and brushed his thumb over the wet side, right by a tiny beetle. Demons killed these little creatures so often, and it tugged at his heart; Rosier knew what it was like to be too small. "And while you're listening to me," he added, "I thought I'd tell you to leave Asmodeus again." The blue beetle skittered over Rosier's nail, then hopped off and away toward another rock. "Or at least to find someone else. You're very beautiful, Rosier. I think any demon would be happy to have you, at least for a night."

Offhandedly, Rosier said, "I'm busy today. I want to make a new tunic." Lucifer said that he'd be happy to ask a demon to make him one. "No, no. I— I'd rather do it myself." He dusted himself off. "I should go now. I'm sorry I couldn't grow any fruits for you."

"For us, Rosier," Lucifer hummed, the sun dipping into the horizon with a ripple of red-orange across the darkening sky. "They're for all of us."

Rosier's cheeks warmed, but his flush wasn't pleasant, more so anxiety-inducing, pressure-hefty. "Yes. I suppose." 'I still don't believe I'm capable of it, but before we fell, I said I wanted us to plant pretty orchards everywhere. I hope that can still happen. I want to share fruits with my friends again.'

As if reading his mind — "I'm sure being in this fruitless place is also responsible for your sadness recently. Once we have some apples, it'll all be better." Satan leaned over to press his lips to his jaw. "You'll see." Against the skin of his friend, he whispered, "Mm. You haven't given yourself horns yet. Many demons have. You should consider that too, duke."

Rosier quirked an eyebrow, but before he could reply, the devil had stepped back and turned on his heel, stalked toward the forestry. A few coos sounded, then a bird landed on Satan's shoulder, speaking to him and fluttering its wings. The buzzes between the ferns called out like they were welcoming him home. 'I can imagine you melting into all the greens, becoming nature itself, friend.' He watched Lucifer leave him silently, and he didn't know why he stared in that direction long after he'd left. He wasn't quite sure either what else to do but go home as he said he would, so Rosier headed for the caves again, away from the coming night.

Upon arrival home, he decided to wash himself with a stone bucket of water, some oils, and a pumice stone. Rosier took all the time in the world to do it, scrubbing at every part of his skin until it reddened and every spec of dirt fell over the cloth he'd set up beneath his stool to soak up the water that dripped from him. He oiled his scalp, then as he waited for his hair to dry — much faster than it used to when it was long — he sat on the floor, legs crossed, and worked at sewing together a new tunic of animal skin. It was very familiar — the threading of flesh together. 'Asmodeus.' He'd thought of him more than a handful of times before and during the washing, and now again, but it was only at this moment that he realized it was certainly time for sleep soon. Would Asmodeus return to him late once more?

'Perhaps, he's going to smell like that again.'

Rosier stared at his craftsmanship — the sewing visibly loose and uneven, the work of a distracted demon. 'Your first bodies were like this too, Asmodeus.' Clumsy and crumbling. Slow, Rosier reeled in as deep of a breath as he could, lifting his gaze toward the silent door, waiting a few seconds more to see if it'd open. When it didn't, he climbed back onto his feet, reaching to fold his half-finished tunic and set it on the table, along with his sewing supplies. 'I should go out looking for him.' He had told Asmodeus long ago not to wander too far or too late, to be next to him often so that he could look after him. 'Maybe he's fallen somewhere and needs me to stop the bleeding.' He had once instructed Asmodeus not to leave his side unless he needed to. 'I'm going to have to tie you to me.' Rosier forced a dry swallow. 'I almost miss when I carried you in a sling.' And Asmodeus could not leave him.

Tepidly, the demon put one foot before the other, both feet bare; he could still remember how soft every floor in Heaven was, even the dirt — but he would forget in time, he was sure. 'I must,' or he would suffer forever. As he pushed aside the entrance, his fingers dragged against the rough boards, and he saw that the corridor was lively but not cramped enough to deter him. Rosier shut the way in behind him before moving along, the demons he passed by flickering their gaze at him, some greeting him, not cruelly exactly but with amusement. Politely, Rosier greeted them back but refrained from asking for Asmodeus' whereabouts for now. He should hopefully be eating; a few times, Asmodeus had gone to eat a little more before bed just to fight weakness. Rosier headed toward the kitchen from the morning then, trying not to look at the others or cause trouble. He stared at his feet, stared at the walls, stared at rooms and peered into a handful, running his eyes over demons smoking, eating, grinding, chattering.

Eventually, he tugged aside a curtain to look into a chamber with a narrow entrance. It was smoky, dark — just the pale glow of some torches lining a wall, bulbs of yellow and orange simmering small; because of this, Rosier squinted, stepped inside, the curtain slipping though his fingers like wind. Sound came to him before vision did. Grunting, grunting. Rosier stared, blinked, took some more steps. Then, there was a rough, rumbling moan like pain, but it was met with sweet, quick gasps for breath. This was not a room, Rosier soon learned, but rather a corridor that led into many smaller rooms like a branch and its limbs; each of these ways was further obscured by either more curtains or doors. From the nearest room, the loudest cries were coming from. And the fallen angel of fruit recognized the voice, of course, of course he did — even as the thumps of his heart rose to his ears like they wanted to muffle his hearing. As Rosier moved toward a wooden door, avoiding the sparse figures in the hall, he noticed a thin opening between the planks.

Impulsively, he shut one eye and peered through with the other. It was only when he saw him — 'Asmodeus' — that he could no longer deny the truth.

On his knees but doubled over, a demon hugged a bulky pillow, pressing his cheek against it, mouth opened wide as a long, purring groan escaped, his eyes half-closed in an utter daze. Meanwhile, Asmodeus' claws were on his hips, and he was barreling into the demon beneath without remorse, rocking him forward harshly against the cushions they were over. Gray trails were steaming from both their lips; there must've been a pipe or joint somewhere, but the crevice in the door wasn't wide enough to allow a viewer to see much of anything beside the two bodies at the center. A great demon of lust, with some of his robe slipping off a shoulder but still mostly dressed, while the one bent over was shamelessly naked, not hiding any pinch of his dark skin.

'He looks like me.' Rosier touched the material of the door before him, felt every dry bristle. 'Though his hair is a little lighter.' His heart felt heavier, though it also felt hollower; at the same time, it was pounding against his front. 'I shouldn't have come looking.' What had he done? 'I already knew this was happening.' And yet, his stomach lurched, and his knees knocked together, and he tightly shut his lips as if to stop something from coming out. What could it be? A scream? A cry?

There was another demon in the room, crawling into view to pepper kisses from the shoulder blade of the one on his hands and knees, trailing along his spine, heading to gnaw at the curves not far from where Asmodeus had buried himself into.

Rosier was shaking, was trying to steady a breath refusing to stay in his lungs, but he didn't move. He watched. He returned to eyeing Asmodeus, who was grunting still with wet beads dribbling down his face, his neck, and along the stitches on his beastly body. 'My friend.' Asmodeus was beautiful, though Rosier had never been the sort to be mystified by beauty — he believed in the beauty of all things — but his friend was beautiful. For a moment, he tried not to think about what had happened between them; he smothered the instinct, the memory of the bed beneath his body, the stare of Asmodeus above his face. He fantasized, pretended he didn't know Asmodeus.

'Who are you?' he lied to himself. 'My name is Rosier. You're frightening, but I can't look away from you.'

When Asmodeus rammed forward, struck a part inside the demon that made him arch his back and let out a noise like a scream, overwhelmed with a trembling, breaking pleasure — Rosier jumped. A snaking warmth crept toward his navel, then below, and his eyes widened a bit. He lifted a hand to the fabric of his clothes by his stomach. 'What is this?' He felt dual sadness, dual nascent desire. Suddenly weak, his legs struggled to hold him up; there was an ache in him like a restricted muscle. 'I should leave.' With a flushed face, Rosier tried to turn back, still listening to every languid, hearty moan. He didn't like this sensation stirring up in him, like steam from water; he was boiling to death.

'I should be happy.' He hurried away, stumbling toward the way he'd come in. 'There's nothing wrong. I already suspected it. All the other demons are doing it, and he hasn't forced himself on me.' Rosier pushed the curtain out of his way, his feet moving quicker and quicker. 'I should be relieved. This is good.' Yet, his eyes were itching, and there was a fire in his throat and some sort of misery pounding at his chest like a visitor at the door. 'I should be happy—' But he was *not*. As the corridor welcomed him, Rosier realized he was just about running. 'Asmodeus will be happy, though, won't he? He's found demons who like sinning with him. And he won't touch me. We can return to how it was between us, before.' He was still thinking of Asmodeus' pleasured groans, of how his body moved forward and back, and his tight grip on that demon's hips. 'We can pretend it never happened.'

"Agh!" a demon shouted and stumbled away from the fallen angel of fruit's sprinting. "Watch where you're running!" But Rosier couldn't hear him.

Later that night, the bed dipped at his side. Rosier twitched awake to it and the sound of canes being set down, then the rustling of someone undressing. This time, Asmodeus smelled clean, but his huffs of pain came in second intervals; he must've overextended himself. Rosier only opened his eyes enough to check if this was a dream — wondering when he'd even fallen asleep — but his friend was soon wrapping his arms around him, holding him tenderly, and the sensation was so encompassing that Rosier couldn't feel anything but that. He touched one of Asmodeus' hands, not far from his chest, with trembling fingers, then scrunched his eyes shut, waiting to be accused of faking sleep, but no such words came. Instead, Asmodeus grunted, his nose pressing against the nape of the fallen angel's neck.

'What am I supposed to do?' Rosier swallowed a shard in his mouth, felt it slice him apart from the inside. 'I shouldn't have seen.' Asmodeus had found others. 'I shouldn't have seen that you've found pleasure elsewhere.' What need did Asmodeus have to return to him ever again? 'But now you won't hurt me.' He should be happy. 'Can we be like before?' No. 'It was wonderful while it lasted. We were wonderful.' Falling meant no more eternity. 'Our love had an end, after all.'

THE SECOND MEMORY

L ight streamed through the opening in the ribs of the mountain. Rosier had not yet remembered how to sleep without curling against someone, against angel Lucifer's corpse — so he was in a fetal position, a gurgling heaviness pressed against his front. It was breathing wetly, managing a coarse groan only a few times a day. Lifting the head, Rosier met Asmodeus' eyes, reddened at the whites, gaze unfocused no matter how many times he blinked. But, before Rosier could say a word to him, dirt crunched beneath someone's feet nearby, and his body flinched on instinct.

'How many times have I had to hide with Lucifer from the likes of angels who wanted to hurt us?' "Rosier," a calm voice called. 'How many times have I hid myself behind a tree to avoid being seen by a mob of the fallen, roaming for blood and for meat and for pleasure?' "Get up." 'Even friends. Even angels who were once friends were among them. I saw them, every time I went out to search for water. I saw them. I ran from them.' "You can't lay there forever." Rosier, finally, began lifting his head. "We no longer have forever."

Face darkened by the light behind him, the reborn devil stood in the gash of the rock, trapping Rosier within the shallow cave, though he was urging him to rise.

"Lucifer?" Rosier whispered, voice hoarse, so devoid of moisture that he could feel the dried cracks within his throat. 'Your voice is almost unrecognizable to me now. I remember how you used to sing and cry in my home in Heaven, but now your words are too firm, too serpentine. Though they've remade you, I can see a red terror on your shadow and at your edges. There is a beast in you. You once told me, and I didn't believe you, but I see it now. When you tilt your head, the light catches on it and sets you aflame. I see the Beast in you now.' "Is something," Rosier whispered, "happening?" Finally, he lowered Asmodeus' decapitated, bleeding head closer to his lap; he held him there often, listening to the constant stream of pain leave his butchered friend's mouth.

"I've decided we need a home, or a center to our new city." Satan took slow, seemingly calculated, steps toward him. In only jewels and glittering chains, his perfect body was entirely exposed, unashamed, though his adornments were so many that he was almost more clothed than Rosier, who wore a mere rag around his waist that had been a tunic once. Only because it had been made with Heaven cotton was it still intact, only by miracle did he still have it in most of one piece, however frayed it had become. "It'll be a mountain that I've already had demons hollow some room in. There isn't much there for now, but I've set aside a place for you."

Rosier stared, every word of the devil echoing; there was a confused kind of uncertainty making the ends of his lips tilt downward, but his mind was fogged enough he could barely untangle his own feelings. "A place for me?"

"I've chosen a select few who will be like princes among demons the way the archangels were among the angels, and these elect will be the first to live within the caves. You're one of them, along with Baal and some others."

"I don't want to be a prince," Rosier whispered, feeling a shiver rattle his bones. "I'm not—"

Satan replied levelly, "If you don't accept the title, then I'll have no reason beyond friendship to have a place for you in the mountain, and I must be careful showing favoritism." Something like a smile formed — but it was too lifeless in Satan's eyes, like a painting of joy by an artist with a tortured hand. "As you know, God didn't declare a favorite until He'd populated most of Heaven. And consider it a gift, many demons wish to be like princes to me, but I've chosen you because you protected my body during my death." Suddenly, he walked again, moving to stand before the fallen angel of fruit and peering down at him, eyes flickering with what might've been sadness but Rosier couldn't tell if that was within the devil's gaze or his own reflecting from empty pupils. "I promised you, in Heaven, that we would create paradise elsewhere."

"There has been," Rosier replied quietly, not knowing why, not knowing if he was arguing, "war. There has been nothing but angels hurting one another on this Earth." He dropped his sight again to the head he'd carried for so long and found his body shivering. "There are so many awful things that I saw. I don't know that I can face any of them again. Even Baal. Even Baal hunted and warred while you were dead. He frightened me. They all frighten me. They will hurt us."

"The sky is clearing, brother, and there will be no more war so long as they follow me. They will no longer be the warring angels but *demons*."

"Will they really follow you?" Rosier's voice was strained, pitched with fright, and breaking, breaking. The urge to tilt his head up and ask God what to do rattled his dull heart, but the Lord hadn't responded to his last few thousand pleas. 'Maybe God is not listening, maybe God is not there to listen.' He set aside that thought immediately. God was there, God was listening — he reassured himself. For many years, he knew, he would continue to pray to God — but you never forget the first time you doubt.

"My other princes are chosen from the greatest warmongers,"

Satan answered, his voice perfectly calm again, like he were only stating the weather. "I will teach them to behave." He took yet another step to stand beside Rosier, then laid a cold hand over his bare shoulder, nearly sending another shudder down the fallen angel of fruit's body. "And they will be loyal to me. They will love me." When Rosier turned up his face, he caught that Lucifer's sight was steady on Asmodeus, his expression stone no matter how much his tongue rolled around the words. "Gather what you have now. There is already a bed for you." Rosier had nearly forgotten what a bed felt like; his life in Heaven had been an eternity, but it all felt like a dream now, the sensations of paradise already leaving him behind. "I won't repeat myself."

"I'm sorry," Rosier surrendered. "I'll do as you say." He breathed in, slow, then asked one final question: "Satan... Lucifer is really dead, isn't he?" But the devil only stared and drifted his hand along Rosier's collarbone, up his throat, working through some of his hair. Then, he left, left Rosier wondering.

CHAPTER 3

Satan made a knowing hum a few days later and said, "You look very sad again." Beneath the sun, he twiddled the thin, emerald stem of yet another never-bloomed fruit. As per usual, Rosier had been trying to coax the petals to reveal pomegranate seeds, but his fingers continued coming back empty, and the flower even began to droop in a wilting sort of sadness. Frowns were rising to the fallen angel of fruit's mouth less often here, however. Disappointment was replaced with expectation and joining the devil most mornings had become part of a routine to get Rosier out of bed that he was thankful for. And, at least, this gave him something to do that wasn't a duty for dukes, which he wasn't. The devil was a charming, entertaining talker, as well. As a young angel, he hadn't been, but Rosier sometimes wondered if that angel Lucifer had ever existed or if he'd been another one of the devil's tricks.

"Oh?" Crouched over the dirt, Rosier turned away from the flowers he'd been focused on to look at the demon standing by his side. "I didn't mean to look that way. I'm sorry." His smile was weak, though he managed a firm voice.

Satan stared at him, this time with no animal on his shoulders, nothing but an embroidered cloak over a thick tunic that fell to his ankles. "Is that true?" His tone was odd, both sincere-sounding and paper thin over something more unrecognizable, maybe distrust. "I'm happy to hear you're well then." Delicately, he reached down to tuck a strand of Rosier's hair behind his ear, then he slipped the end of a flower there. "In that case, I'd like to ask you for a favor. Is that alright?"

"It is," Rosier replied, looking to the not-quite-a-lily in his periphery. "If I can be any help, I don't mind at all."

"Well, I needed Baal to come bring me a couple hundred animal corpses. I'm hoping for a feast for the solstice in a few months, and I believe preparations this far ahead are in order. I think some demons are interested in getting some horns as well. Rosier, you should tell Baal what kind of horns you'd like, or you can go out hunting with him and choose."

Frowning, the fallen angel of fruit replied, "I don't really have much of an interest in having horns."

"But, Rosier, you still look like an angel."

"You do too, Lucifer," Rosier said levelly, his brows stitched together with a flicker of confused hurt, but Satan laughed.

"I only look like I did before I fell," said Satan, "and I never quite looked like an angel, did I? I was too beautiful for it. You could say I looked like God." Rosier didn't really think that. "But don't look so sad again. I'm just trying to help, Rosier." Gently, now, the devil took Rosier's hand and tugged him up and onto his feet, then he squeezed his fingers. "Now, can you go and speak to Baal for me, as I asked?"

Rosier swallowed his nerves, focusing on the perfect fingers of his perfect friend. "Yes, Lucifer." What other choice did he have? Slowly, he stepped away, allowing himself to escape Satan's touch, to head for the caves again. He realized he hadn't been alone with Baal in a long time, maybe since the creation of Asmodeus' first bodies. Most often, Rosier saw Baal in groups or, at the very least, with Asmodeus. This wouldn't be the first time that Rosier called upon Baal to slaughter and bring him dead animals, but he hated to remember. Regardless, he did.

The darkness of the caves was both a comfort and punishment — the same way that hiding from the skies and the eyes of God was — but if nothing else, it was familiar now. Rosier did like the forestry outside, especially in comparison to the halls overbrimming with sin, but for now, the fruitless branches were frustrating him. Perhaps, he should go out further one day, see the rest of the healed Earth. After the fruits, maybe. There were some demons who wandered out to the very ends of the planet, enjoying their freedom, and for now, Satan allowed it. As long as they still worshiped him, he allowed it. He seemed perfectly fine to allow anything, so long as he was worshiped.

Finding Baal proved to require asking a few strangers, most who groaned at the name of their tormentor. "Baal," they sighed. "Baal," they grumbled. "He was beating Mammon earlier for disobeying orders, and he wouldn't stop until Mammon lost several teeth. Yesterday, he choked Ishtar until his eyes were bulging out of his skull." They called him a monster, the horrible beast that stood at the side of their sweet, loving devil. But — all these demons did point Rosier in the direction of a lounge, one not too far from the deep heart of the cave system — Satan's chambers. Past a rock archway, it revealed itself to be rather decorated as far as unimportant rooms went: the walls were painted with flames, genitals, and weapons, and there were three divans with feathered blankets draped over them, and a low table was holding many opaque bottles of what were almost certainly an array of fermented drinks, alcohols but nothing like the Heaven variety yet.

There were a few demons in the room, most notably Baal, who was seated, though asleep. With his burly arms crossed and his head leaned back with great horns nearly scrapping the wall, his mouth was wide open to trickle out snores, not very loud but not quite so subdued either. The sight was enough for Rosier's lips to twitch in a faint smile at the memory of the angel of flight in Heaven, but that fraction of joy lasted no more than a second. Before long, the vision of angel Baal was obscured by that of a great demon, dripping viscera and smiling brilliantly as the Earth burned all around him; in the fields of war against fallen angels and the remaining beasts, he'd been at home; among the dead, he'd only looked hungry. Rosier never did understand what happened to Baal. He only knew that, during the war in Heaven, his old friend had turned away from him as the rebel angels forged weapons and armored themselves to take on their Creator, but what had Lucifer done to turn Baal against God?

Now, Rosier found himself taking some steps toward him, touching his arm, and whispering his name.

When the fallen angels had found Lucifer's corpse on Earth, Baal had been at Rosier's side, had grieved the most gorgeous angel with a wail of agony like so many others. He had offered his jewelry, and he had aided in the remaking of Lucifer's divine beauty. And when the wars on Earth had begun, Baal positioned himself as a great authority, as one of the closest friends of their dead messiah — except Rosier soon saw how Baal's gaze fell onto Lucifer with the same glint as all the others. Something impatient, something *wanting*.

Baal grunted, opened one eye, then the other. "Hgh?" A good-natured and rumble of a laugh seeped from a growing smile. "Rosier, I haven't seen you in weeks." Really, it had only been a few days.

Nodding without reason, Rosier replied, "Lucifer sent me. He wants you to bring back a few hundred animals for the solstice. Some demons are interested in horns, so you should make sure not to break any." He spoke gently, sweetly; he still enjoyed trying kindness. Every instance that he could be kind was like returning to Heaven, he thought.

With another gruff noise, the duke planted his feet on the ground but didn't stand yet. "Did he tell you by when he needs them?"

"Well," said Rosier, "by the solstice, I imagine."

Baal laughed again, this time louder. "Very wise of you, duke. I'll try to have some corpses in here within a few days if I can yell at enough demons to lend me their help." His head tilted to Rosier, then he quirked an eyebrow. "What are you frowning about?"

"I don't really like to be called that." Rosier shifted from one foot to the other, turning his face toward the way he'd come. "I don't think I'm a duke. Or I don't want to be."

Snorting — "You should tell Satan that."

"He frightens me," Rosier murmured, "at times."

"For me, it's all the time," Baal joked. "But I love it. I love him."

Rosier answered softly, "How can you love someone you're so afraid of?"

"That was how we loved God, wasn't it? Fearfully?" However profound those words could have been, they were watered down by the amused twist at one of the ends to Baal's mouth, whose lips were curling up into a toothy smile.

Someone else called out, "Baal, you're awake!" with such sharpness that both Baal and Rosier startled and twisted their heads in the same direction, watching as a demon who'd been at the other side of the room sauntered over slowly — a blonde with a tunic and fur coat as well as sandals that were laced high onto his legs. "I've been waiting on that for hours now. Can you try to listen to me for a moment?"

Immediately, Baal sighed and said, "I don't have the time for fucking right now, Gemory."

"Oh, quiet," Gemory replied, planting a hand on his hip. "This has nothing to do with our cocks in each other's mouths. I'm here on behalf of my friends. Your friend Moloch has been going around and hurting demons for no reason again. Last week, he told my Seir that he needed to talk to him, something about duke duties, and then once they were alone, Moloch raped him and threatened to hurt him if he told anyone."

Baal pressed his lips together into a fine line in frustration, and almost boredom, even though Rosier had flinched. "And what are you telling me this for?"

"Because," Gemory snapped, "he's going around doing whatever he likes and saying Satan has blessed him to do it. Well, I won't stand for my friends being abused any longer, and if Satan or you other dukes don't stop this, then what purpose is there in living here? The Earth is massive, and other demons are whispering about finding another mountain." He paused, then added, quieter: "And I'm sure Satan wouldn't like to hear that Moloch claims he has the devil's full support."

"I hope your friend is okay," Rosier interjected, his voice unsteady. "Seir, was it? If he needs anything— If I can offer anything—"

"Dismember Moloch," replied Gemory with an irritated huff. "That's all Seir wants and that's all I can think of that would help. You're a duke too, aren't you? Why don't *you* do something about it? Punish him. That's what you dukes do."

Rosier stared, thinking to shake his head and negate this sudden responsibility on his shoulders, but Baal thankfully spoke up: "I'll talk to Satan about it." He exhaled through his nose harshly and shook his head. "Tonight. Or tomorrow. Trust that I'd love to beat the fuck out of him, but a duke fighting with another is forbidden. It's the only rule Satan gives us besides worshiping him. So, I'll ask him what we can do."

Gemory breathed, slow and in enough relief to dip his shoulders. "Good. I'm glad *someone* will listen to me."

"In the meantime, stay out of his way. Tell him you're doing something for me. Tell Seir to do the same." Baal set his hands on his knees, then finally reeled himself up to stand with a low noise of strain. "As if I don't have enough shit to deal with." He turned back to Rosier and nodded his chin at him. "You see, Lucifer probably sent you because he's angry I accidentally finished on his face last night." Instantly, Rosier felt his stomach twist; he was getting better at living with the idea that his friends were fornicating, though it still made him uncomfortable to be updated on it. "But at least this'll distract him from that."

Gemory laughed heartily, his demeanor finally brightening

up as he lifted a hand to cradle one of his cheeks, while the other held his elbow. "That reminds me of how annoyed Asmodeus was this morning after I spilled too fast. You would think they'd take it as a compliment, wouldn't you?" 'Asmodeus?' Rosier felt the beats of his heart stutter and lose rhythm. "He forgot about it quickly, though."

Baal replied: "Oh, is that where Asmodeus has been?"

"He was fucking me and a few others for hours by the pools." Gemory waved the hand by his face. "There's no satisfying him at all, but he never runs out of willing partners. He's very good, probably one of the best fucks I've had." Rosier was feeling his heart fall now, like it'd been snipped from a string and left to collapse into his stomach. "I'm not the possessive type, but I can't help but be jealous of whoever he shares his bed with."

"Excuse me," Rosier blurted, the words like scalpels shredding their way out his mouth. "I need to return to my chamber now. " His steps backward were unsteady, but just as he felt himself tripping, he turned around, hurried toward the door, and ignored the inquisitive noise that the large duke was making behind him, as well as Gemory asking Baal who Rosier was, what his issue might be. 'Don't tell him that I share a bed with Asmodeus. Don't tell him anything.' But he dared not to stay and listen and hope. His feet moved so fast beneath him that they blurred, and all the air in his lungs was running out of his mouth.

He thought of Asmodeus, surround by bodies, making them cry out in pleasure like he'd seen recently. He imagined it, so vividly that he might as well have been there to smell and hear every second of it. To see his friend's dark eyes stare at him over the shoulder of a demon he's rolling his hip into, to see him snickering, saying, 'Look at what you refused to give me. Do you think I'm going to keep returning every night to you after you denied me on the only night that mattered? There are so many other beds open for me. Watch, Rosier.'

Arriving to his chambers, Rosier scurried in and slammed the door in place behind him, his chest rising and falling with pants that were, frankly, overdramatic for the distance he'd run. He placed a hand over half of his face, blinding an eye, trying to call himself back from his thoughts that were all incoherent emotion rather than any reasonable words. What was this? Why was he upset? Why was he upset?! He'd told himself to be happy because Asmodeus had found demons who enjoyed being fucked. But his throat itched and his eyes burned, and his feet dragged as he moved toward his bed.

'How can I feel so hurt?' His body pulsed like misery was his new heart, and he doubled over like a flower in drought. Rosier set a knee at the end of the bedding, then climbed onto it, fisting his hands into the pillows to wrench himself out of the sinkhole of worry in his head, but it did nothing to calm him. 'Asmodeus, why are you doing this?' He knew why. 'Can't you simply live without fucking? For me, for your darling Rosier?' After all, Asmodeus had lived that way for billions of years in Heaven; he'd waited billions of years. Why should Asmodeus have to return to the chaste touches and innocent kisses? He must be terribly happy to have desire and to be finally able to fulfill it.

'I have desire too.' Rosier choked up, droplets beginning to dribble down to his soft cheeks, and all he could do was clench his eyes shut. 'I swear that I do. I desire you, Asmodeus. But maybe not enough.'

The door opened. And the fallen angel of fruit startled, body jerking upward before he twisted his face back to see the very demon he'd been shedding tears so immaturely for. Pulling the wooden-slabs back into place over the exit, Asmodeus' eyes, a bit rounder than they ever were, fell on him, and as he limped closer, he revealed himself to only be using one walking aid that he hastily set aside, dangerously close to their hearth. "Rosier?" left his mouth just as he staggered to the side of the bed, climbed onto it; his voice was quiet, almost like a tender caress or a tender bruise. "What's wrong?" His touch fell, delicate, over Rosier's arm.

Blinking rapidly, inhaling unsteady and weak, Rosier

noticed the cold sensation of dried tear trails down his face, feeling them streak down to his neck and even to his collarbone. The pained sound of his name came once more and left the fallen angel no other choice but to drift his gaze to the face of the demon he'd half-created, laying now on his hip, staring with curved, worried brows and a mouth pressed shut anxiously.

Once again, it was just the two of them in the bedroom. It always did return to this. Rosier in bed, waiting for his beloved friend, who was with his lovers. The sun always rose.

"Asmodeus?" Rosier wasn't sure why called for him like this, like he didn't know who he was, like he'd never met him. "What's wrong?" He lifted tired fingers and brought them to push away a strand of Asmodeus' hair that was slicing his face in half. "You look sad."

"Rosier," Asmodeus answered, "were you crying?"

He wanted to lie, but Rosier didn't want to sin, didn't want to be a demon. "If I was, I'm not anymore."

"Can you tell me why you were?" Asmodeus looked so nice today; he often wore easily removable robes, but he was currently in a long, crimson tunic and many jewels embracing his neck, his arms, dangling from his ears and tall horns. With the hand that hadn't drifted to the bedding beside Rosier's shoulder, he took the younger demon's cheek, dragging a thumb against the ghost rivulets on brown skin. "Can't you tell me what's wrong? You've been upset for some time."

At such affection, Rosier could've easily forgotten why he'd been crying, but Asmodeus had that smell on him again — sweat and semen. "I'd rather sleep right now."

"I don't," came Asmodeus' careful words, "want you to stay in bed for days again." Again. "Are you sure you don't want to tell me? Should I have Lucifer come talk to you?"

"I'm sorry," Rosier whispered the same way he'd done on the day he'd begun cutting corpses for Asmodeus' head. "Can you hold me?"

"Yes, but I should wash first. Do you mind? I think I might need some stitches replaced soon."

Rosier was relieved, in fact. "I don't mind at all." A soft, sweet smile trailed along his lips. "I'll wait for you. Then we can both sleep." Asmodeus' chuckle was fond. "Go on."

What was he crying about? Asmodeus was being accommodating, was still willing to hold him every night. That was all Rosier wanted. He wanted to kiss his friend softly on the lips and feel his arms around him, and he wanted their legs to tangle, their noses to nuzzle. 'Why can't I be happy then?' He began to wonder if he did want to fuck him, if he wanted to be bent over a pillow like that demon he'd seen the other day, Asmodeus driving into him over and over, but just the thought was enough to make him grimace.

Even still — 'Why did I ever react that way in Heaven? Am I in the wrong? Maybe I should have taken his kisses and his hands sliding along my legs, his curious fingers. Why didn't I let myself take it? Was I scared?'

Rosier considered this as Asmodeus went for their washing bucket, oils, and stone, then stepping in front of the hearth. Before he washed, he lit a fire, and though there wasn't any part of Asmodeus' body that Rosier wasn't familiar with, he decided to watch. He thought of how, as angels, nudity had been nothing special and the bathhouse had been innocent and lovely. Rosier could still remember sitting on the edge of the pool, working soap through his hair, staring at his Asmodeus laughing and talking with another angel as they washed. What had done this to their bodies? What had turned them from something so pure to something to be ashamed of?

Asmodeus, soon, was wholly undressed; he had the body of a beast, of many beasts. And, though Rosier had just insisted there was desire in him, there was little of it in this moment. He barely caught the shadow and scent of Asmodeus bringing a roll of herbs to his mouth to smoke before exhaustion pulled him under.

THE THIRD MEMORY

Curled up around Asmodeus' head, Rosier laid on a sack of leaves, in darkness, and with an animal skin blanket over his figure. His tunic was still bloodied from that morning, but he didn't think of it, didn't want to anymore. "I miss you." He nuzzled his face against the top of Asmodeus' head, then smiled sadly when his friend gurgled against him, the sound wet and strained as tearing hem. "You will be okay." It felt nice to say. "You will be okay." He tilted him upward and then pecked his warm, dead mouth. "You will see that all will be better soon. It's nicer in here than it was out there. It's quieter." He paused, feeling the red on Asmodeus' lips drag against his own. "My friend."

He was remembering again Asmodeus' empty eyes that night in Heaven, the only night in Heaven. The feeling of his friend's arousal, pressing against him like someone hiding a dagger beneath their clothes, already damp with blood. 'Are you alright?' he'd asked. 'Why are you looking at me like that?' My friend, my brother. 'You're frightening—' too-sharp fingers dragging up against his clothing '—me.' Then, Asmodeus' face had been against his throat, hot, breathing slow enough that it raked down Rosier's body. Tongue followed, hot and dripping up to his ear.

'What are you doing?' He would never remember if he told him to stop or not. There would be times that he believed that he did want it, and he was mistaking regret for never having wanted his touch at all. Memory is as fallible as the heart that conjures it. After all, his legs had jerked for a moment because of an unfamiliar goodness tightening at his core and pulsing awake; if he hadn't been liking it, then why had he felt that? For a second, certainly, he had leaned into his mouth and tried to see if he could grow firm in need as well.

Today, he was lying to himself, and he was happy Asmodeus had done what he did. Tomorrow, he will hate him again. There is love there always, only sometimes bundled in angry grief. If he didn't love him, it would not hurt this much, would it?

"There are some demons," Rosier whispered to his friend in the dark, "that have taken from the bodies of beasts what they lost — arms, legs. I'm sure you've seen it too." The urge to kiss him again returned, but the taste of silver was twisting his stomach. "I saw them. Earlier." He'd watched the dukes set a furred creature onto the stone table between them, a thrashing thing of paleness; it could have been a lamb, though it was too horned. 'They killed it.' The demons. 'Pulled it apart until strings held it together. God is strings; I know it now.' Then, the chief prince of the demons — Baal — had brought an obsidian dagger down onto its body. 'It's looking to me. Oh, poor thing, don't look at me.' Rosier was almost drowning among the crowd of fallen angels, and there was yet another suffocation in his throat, as he found it tougher, denser to breathe each time. Tears were scorching the inside of his skull, but only one, or two, leaked out of him. 'No, don't look at me.' The bleating, darling, confused creature.

'You want me to save you. I can't. I can't.' The animal had jerked with each stab that wretched out a new rope of red, untangling to pool. In a splatter, the blood itself reached out to claw at Rosier's tunic, and the soul in its gaze maintained itself on the fallen angel of fruit's face. 'I can't save you. Forgive me.' He had witnessed death already, countless times during the wars on Earth — the initial dying, all the mass slaughter in chaos afterward, and then the targeted attacks as the dust settled — but he had never dared to stand so close. 'I'm helpless here. My hands are tied even if they are holding a head. I can't help. I can't save you.' What kind of angel couldn't save a soul crying for help? Perhaps that's why he'd fallen. Heaven is for the good, Earth is for the wicked, and Hell is for those who see them both but do nothing.

One demon tore the horns off the creature and fixed them to his own head.

"I could," Rosier whispered, "create a body for you."

THE FOURTH MEMORY

"You can't keep carrying that thing around."

Rosier twitched, only then realizing where he was — on something of a cushion, against something of a wall, though it was too curved inward and too unevenly lumped against his back. Dry, a breath trickled from between his lips, and his head turned to see the devil there, his hands together at his front, his bracelets fine, golden loops that cascaded down his forearms. Half his face was deeply shadowed as he stood beside a torch whose obsidian handle had been screwed to the wall. Its burning was quiet, and for a flame, it was rather too still, like it feared the king of all the fallen at its side. Rosier, too, felt his tired hands on the head he cradled stiffen. "Mm? What are you... referring to?"

"That head."

"Asmodeus?"

Behind Satan, there were some dark figures, other demons approaching, but he maintained his cold stare on the ruined angel of fruit. "Go and cut him a body, out of trees or out of animals. What are you waiting for? Do you think the angels will toss us his body? It's already gone. Burnt. If there's any of it left in Heaven, then it's beyond healing. Cut him some limbs to use or leave him in the woods." As Rosier tried to speak, or perhaps just take another breath — "I'm sure you've seen others in the caves that have remade themselves with animal meat. Go out and kill for it. I can't stand to see you carry that head around any longer. You're no help as a duke if you're more concerned with the hair of that thing than doing as I say." 'I don't want to be a duke.' "Or would you rather Asmodeus continue to suffer?"

At this, Rosier felt his fingers thread a little too tightly into the bundled braids he'd pinned to the back of his friend's skull. "I —" His heart nearly fell from his mouth. "I've already thought of that." He stared at his own bare feet, idly rocking his heel against the hard, cold stone. Though it had been years now since they'd moved into the caves, and now there were two hundred, at least, living among the channels, Rosier was still trying to accustom to the hollow coolness of the place and wore a thicker robe he had to resist shivers in. "But I don't think I could do it, Lucifer." He still called him that, each time expecting to be punished, but Satan never corrected him, though he often corrected many others. "I don't think that I could—"

"Shame," interjected the devil, so sudden that Rosier, briefly, thought he was merely naming the emotion in the fallen fruit angel's chest. "Toss him away then. There are duties you must attend to, and that head is distracting."

"It's Asmodeus," Rosier tried to say. "Isn't he our friend?"

"Toss him," repeated Satan, then turned his back without another word, brushing past the two demons that had stepped up behind him — Baal and the red-haired Moloch. The latter didn't hesitate to follow, just about spinning on his heel and calling after him, while Baal, strangely, lingered, only following Satan with his gaze before facing Rosier again. There was a tugging over his mouth — something that seemed a frown whereas his eyes were wide with excess thinking. It'd been perhaps centuries since Baal and Rosier had spoken at length, the last few times littered with Rosier's fear and Baal's anger. Baal demanding to see the Lucifer Rosier was hiding away, and the smaller one shaking his head until he was sure it'd roll off and he'd join Asmodeus as a mere skull. 'No. No, Baal. You frighten me. I won't let you touch him — Y-You're just like all the others, though you don't realize it. Please don't hurt him—' And, for now, the two continued their silence, Baal twisting away to chase after his beloved king.

But the two of them — Rosier and Baal — did speak again, just a few days later.

It was true that Rosier couldn't muster the strength to butcher any of the animals that he saw and stitch together something new. In fact, he couldn't even manage catching them, and after a few tries running after small mammals, he realized that if he didn't want Asmodeus to suffer any longer, and he didn't want Satan to scold him again, then help was required. The devil, after all, was right that enough time had passed and that the angels above hadn't found the empathy to fling down the remains of either Asmodeus' body or anyone else's. Rosier didn't, however, want to face Lucifer again — realizing now that Satan may even prefer Asmodeus to be *tossed* rather than fixed — and, further complicating things, whenever he peered out into the narrow corridors, Rosier only saw unfamiliar monsters and violence and fucking. He saw a lot of fucking; it was so frequent that he began to feel out of place. 'Even after the Earth wars have ended, they're still interested in this violent, dirty act?'

Walking along, he'd found Baal doing just that — fucking. He had a demon on his lap, gripping his hips and rocking up into him. Just as the demon went to graze his teeth at the duke's ear, Baal's eyes fell on Rosier, and he just about jumped, before the fallen fruit angel staggered to spin around, gripping the sling where he held Asmodeus, to scramble back the way he came. He'd only traveled down a few corridors before he heard Baal's shouts, calls of his name, and Rosier stopped, though he didn't turn. Staring at the demons ahead of him, there were some embracing, some entranced by gossip.

"Rosier," Baal continued to say. "Wait." The fallen angel of fruit lowered his face, realizing that the burly demon could still speak without snarling. "I heard what Satan said to you. He told you to make Asmodeus a body. I can help." Rosier still refused to meet his eyes. "I miss him. He was my friend too." And so Baal took the initiative once more, stepping closer and around Rosier and looking down at him; he had enormous horns now, jutting from his head to curve upward at the very ends. "Will you let me?"

What other choice did he have? "Yes. Yes, I would— I would really appreciate any help. Thank you."

"Of course." He lifted a hand, not yet clawed, then touched some of Asmodeus' braided hair; the head was facing Rosier's chest. "I'll go out and help you collect some animals. I'll kill them for you, if you need." He paused, then added softer: "I was curious about something else, too. I wanted to ask— What ever did happen to Asmodeus during the war in Heaven? Whatever happened between the two of you?"

Rosier chose not to answer; Baal didn't ask again. Within a few days, the two of them ventured out of the caves into the forestry, the trees excessively tall, their roots tangled into soil still marred by the apocalypse of angel fall — scorched creatures and plants alike. It was all different from how it had been when the beasts ruled the Earth, but it was not worse, at least Rosier hoped not. He laid a hand on some bark and watched his friend take animals — at this moment in time, there were only some leftover beasts and mammals swelling in size — and wrench them closer to himself before lifting a stone axe. Bringing it down once, then again, each time spurring less spasms from the dying life at his fingertips. Almost always, Rosier would screw his eyes painfully shut like that would be enough for this not to be happening. Like not looking would be enough not to hear the shrieks of terror and panic.

Baal spoke with him as they continued down the mountain. "Lucifer still speaks kindly to you. I'm happy about that. He's very different now. He's become... unfamiliar, but I don't mean that negatively. No, no. Not at all. He feels like another creature all together now. Like God. He's like God to me. I love him."

"I love him too," Rosier relented, caressing the head he carried in a sling.

"He doesn't want to fuck me. I don't know why. He barely allows me to kiss his ankles. Yesterday, he called me into his room, and he ordered me to dress him. He could feel me shaking, I think." Rosier wanted to ask him to stop talking, but he nibbled on his bottom lip instead. "He must've known what I was thinking. He looked at me like he knew. And then he... stared at me for a while. Like he was waiting. I haven't decided yet if he wanted me to take him, after all, or if he was hoping I would try so that he could punish me for it. I was on my knees. I told him that he was beautiful. He lifted a foot, then he put it on my head, and he told me to say it again." Uneasily, the fallen angel of fruit swallowed. "Oh, I see another creature. There. I'll kill it quickly."

With an animal-skin pouch hanging over his shoulder, Baal lugged the couple corpses back, not complaining, not even asking for any help. Rosier was thankful for it at the same time that he was ridden with guilt. But it was the right decision, for once they stepped into Rosier's chambers, and Baal began to pick out the bodies, hanging in broken, bent limpness, Rosier felt his stomach almost yank itself out through his mouth. Such nausea had him stumble as he ordered Baal to leave at the same time he brought his shaking hands to cleavers prepared in advance. "Rosier," Baal called, as he had days ago. "Are you certain?"

"Please," Rosier pleaded, trying to steady his thinking, but the stench of bodies that hadn't even rotted yet was in his nose, in his mouth. "I want to do this alone." There were a few beats of silence. "I beg you." More silence, then he heard the thumps of steps, moving toward the door, and he stared at the head of Asmodeus that he'd propped up on the bed and noticed how his friend's eyes followed the demon heading out. Rosier tightened his grip on the butchering tool in his hands, then he stepped toward the creatures and began.

The first time, of the many that will follow, was a gory, horrible spectacle. Rosier was so slow in dismembering each of the dozen collected bodies that the process took days, days wherein rot began to take hold of the skin and its hidden meat. Swatting away at insects — doing so bewildered because Rosier hadn't dealt with so many critters like this since he lived outside the caves — he tried to focus on the softest sections to remove first. Except, each instance that Rosier dug in to chip at bone, he'd feel a tremor rack his body. Days without food, he was beginning to feel weaker, and he had hardly the strength to take Asmodeus' head, lug it over, and hastily attach it with too-large stitchings to a conglomerate of mismatched limbs and furs. "Asmodeus," he tried, "will this be enough?" He echoed it, heard his voice in all its fear. "Can you make this your body?"

A single, jarring twitch of the bloody mass replied; then, clumsy stitches at the abdomen ripped and viscera spilled onto the stone at the same moment Asmodeus' mouth opened in a gurgled, wordless groan of agony.

Rosier, instantly, took the threads at the throat and ripped them off, intending to take his friend and kick away the body, but he was soon staggering backward. With a gasp, he instinctively touched his chest only to smear red over the white of his clothes. A spiral of dizziness struck him next, and he saw the ground approaching him before he felt its hardness against his knees, then his side. His heaving turned hot; the shakes of his head grew fast enough to blind him. To Asmodeus, he cried, "No. Forgive me. I didn't mean to hurt you." Gasps, gasps. "I can't *help you.*"

Yet, the door was creaking open a mere few seconds later, and as Rosier jerked his head in the direction, he saw Baal, his mouth open, like he was going to say he'd forgotten something last time he was here or he wanted to check in on the state of his old friend. "What—" He froze, and he looked at the mess of abominated, decomposing bodies around them. "Rosier—" Stepping in, pulling the door shut behind him, he hurried toward the fallen angel of fruit who tried to jump away from him.

"No," Rosier rasped, nearly hissed. "Don't touch me— I've done something terrible. I've made a beast. With my own hands, *I've created a beast.*" Baal, as asked, didn't touch him, but he immediately stared back at the meat over the stone and the — *drip, drip* — blood from where the stitching had torn. He stared at Asmodeus' heaving face, as well, flushed but doing no more than gasping and groaning. Then, Baal's face twisted in what could have been read as disgust but was really pity, almost guilt, as if he were responsible, 'even though I am the only one here who needs to confess.' "I don't know," Rosier continued in a low drawl, "how to live having done this. I'm not like you or the others."

Under his breath, Baal answered, "I'll bring Lucifer," but Rosier shook his head once more. "He'll be able to help."

"Please don't, Baal." He didn't want to see the true Beast of Heaven and Earth. "Please."

Baal did touch him now, his shoulder, but no matter how gentle his fingers were, Rosier's trembling refused to still. "I'll wait here with you." Hasty, the fallen angel of fruit brought a hand to one of his own eyes and attempted to rub the itch away from it. "Once you've calmed, I'll go for him." Rosier hadn't known Baal could still speak so gently; he hadn't known this demon had any memory of his past angel life. "Would that be better for you?" Then, Baal smiled, warmly, familiarly, like a fallen angel of home.

"Yes," Rosier found himself saying, allowed himself to lean into his old friend. 'How long has it been since anyone has held me up?' "Thank you... Baal."

After this, there was silence, until Rosier's breathing had slowed into a steadier rhythm, and Baal gave his shoulder a final, firm squeeze. For the first time since the war for Heaven, Rosier had the urge in him to call someone brother. 'Brother Baal.' And he decided to sit still as Baal left him; he decided to fiddle with his bloodied hands, and not look at his decapitated friend nearby, until the devil arrived alone.

CHAPTER 4

For some weeks, the fallen angel of fruit returned to bearing no fruit. Satan now entertained himself with other things — threads and tools, all for embroidering, weaving, carving — as Rosier made his several daily attempts at creation. Sometimes, he tried talking to Lucifer. "How have you been?" Rosier liked to ask. "How are all the demons?" The answer was always prompt, simple, and even honest. One day, he went on talking too much and said, "I do wonder at times what has become of Michael." With a twig, he fiddled and fiddled. "I never did understand what happened—" Satan wasn't answering, so he turned his face and saw the devil sitting with an animal bone necklace he was tying the ends of. "I remember when you introduced him to me. He came by the house, and you two went to your room."

'I wondered what you did. I thought that maybe you were doing what all angels do — resting, playing, wrestling, talking. But knowing what I do now, I can't help but think that maybe you were pleasing one another. I wonder if that is how it all came to be — if you, Lucifer, with Michael, learned that angels can kiss all we like on the mouth and become one and create on our own, create *sin*.' But then why would the chief prince Michael betray

Lucifer, the favorite of God? Rosier didn't understand. 'Isn't love like worship? What could ever make a lover stop believing?'

"You remember too much," Satan said, his voice shockingly uninterested, not at all enraged as one might have expected. "Don't speak of that time." Then, sharper — "Don't speak of that angel either."

"Forgive me," Rosier said, quietly, turning away and staring at the sky, the clouds, noticing how soft they looked. 'Oh to fly again...' "I didn't mean to upset you. I only ask because you're my friend, and I spent too long in Heaven pretending there was nothing harming you. So I suppose—" Selfishly, Rosier thought of what had happened to him. "I was curious if Michael ever hurt you." It would make sense, wouldn't it? Michael had loved Lucifer, then hurt him. 'Asmodeus loved me, then hurt me too.'

"What does it matter if he did?" was the response. "If you think that there is any liking I still harbor for the archangel of God, then know that there is none. I hope that he is suffering, and that he has seen where cowardice leads him. There is no love left in me, nor is there even pity."

"But you... did love him once?" Rosier wasn't sure why he asked. All of Heaven, all of Earth, knew that Michael and Lucifer had loved each other once. We are all living in the grave of their love.

"I was young, then." And the conversation ended there. The two went on a walk, afterward, to the river again, then they foraged some herbs to eat.

Another day, Rosier tried, "What about Baal and you?" When it came to Baal, Lucifer always huffed, called him simple-minded and idiotic — only then to admit he'd been eating with him before arriving to the garden. "I think... Baal is kind even if he hides it now. He terrified me during the wars here on Earth, but he's become a little gentler since, at least to me. I was remembering the other day how he brought me all those animals that I used to create Asmodeus' first body."

Sitting on a cushion this time, Lucifer was working a strand through some linen — he was decorating his summer clothes — as he hummed; the solstice was soon. "Right. I remember how I had to guide your hand to make you dismember those beasts." Rosier's lips twitched; what a terrible memory that was. "I lost my patience and shouted at you, didn't I?" Satan had snarled, the disguise of his beauty almost slipping, as Rosier cried that he didn't want to hurt the beasts, even if they were already dead. "You couldn't understand that they wouldn't feel the pain anymore."

Rosier was crouched by some dandelions nearby but looking straight at the devil, whose blonde hair tangled with the breeze. "I still don't really understand." He was remembering Satan beginning to dig his nails into his wrists, snapping at him to stop crying and being so fragile and afraid.

"I told you that you were a demon now," Lucifer mused, "and that demons don't cry. God creates, and demons kill. Demons sin. They can't be weak."

Almost in a whisper, Rosier asked, "I'm still weak, aren't I?"

"You're not done maturing," Lucifer murmured, more distantly. "You told me how fruits mature when I was young. One day, you'll be stronger. Ripe for a demon." A faint smile curled over his plump lips. "I have patience." The word didn't make Rosier feel much better; he didn't like the idea of anyone waiting on who he might become; why couldn't he be loved the way that he is now? "You're much better at making new bodies for Asmodeus now, aren't you?" Rosier made a noise of affirmation. "I've been telling you to teach him how to repair himself. Look how far you've come. And Asmodeus is far behind. You're a duke."

Rosier wanted to change the subject. "That first body of his was horrible, wasn't it?" That parody of an angelic body, that mass of limbs and meat. "He's never told me how much it hurt, but I think it was a lot. I still feel guilty."

"You don't think he deserved it?"

The sound of Asmodeus' rough, guttural scream of pain

echoed in the cave of his skull, and the wet squelch of muscles seizing, then the tearing of the stitches. Spilling, splattering, red and rot.

"I don't think," Rosier whispered, "anyone deserves suffering."

Satan laughed. "Not even me?"

At some moment, he must've turned to look at the flowers again, their yellow petals so bright he felt as if he were staring at a hundred suns, as if he were in the skies again, not on Earth. "No. Never you, Lucifer. You could do anything, and I still wouldn't think you deserve suffering."

The devil made a gruff, irritated noise. "If you don't hurt those who've hurt you, then they'll keep doing it. They'll never stop. They'll beat you until you break. Do you want that?" No sound of a reply or even a breath. "One day, you'll understand, but the others can be so right of you, at times: you act too much like an angel."

Tepidly, Rosier decided to ask, "How can I stop? How can I stop being an angel?"

"Fall," was the answer. In love or out of love — but fall.

But Rosier didn't. He rose to his feet, instead, and he headed toward his old friend to wish him a farewell for now. Satan accepted the kiss on the cheek, then whispered for him to rest with a reborn, but perhaps shallow, kindness. This, Rosier, decided to disobey too. As he left him, he thought to act on an impulse he'd had since the morning after Asmodeus had caught him crying. He returned to the caves, curling his hands into fists as he clutched at his robes. 'Should I try searching for him by the kitchens? By the theater?' He remembered the room where he'd seen Asmodeus fornicating the first time except he couldn't recall the labyrinth way he'd arrived there.

As was always the case, the corridors were dense — demons in talk, shoving playfully, flaunting new clothes or new malformations screwed along their bodies. Some were pressed to a wall, mouths locked, hands roaming. Rosier briefly wondered what that would be like, to be pinned to stone and touched. He had been pinned to a bed once; he hadn't liked it. 'I don't know what I like.' He was young, then, and scared, too young. 'But I could be ripe now,' he hoped and continued on his way, inhaling carefully, looking and even catching a demon or two who snickered at the too-angelic being among them. Not allowing that to stray his focus, Rosier bit on the inside of his cheeks and tried to smile in response.

In fact, he even approached them, watching one's face melt into a surprised flush as he asked if they knew where Asmodeus was. The one less flustered replied with a sluggish point down a hall and some simple directions. It was quite a different way than the one Rosier remembered he'd seen Asmodeus having sex in last time, but he knew that demons seemed keen to pleasure one another anywhere they liked. So, he nodded his head and expressed some thanks as he turned, trying to let a scornful response fall on deaf ears. Making his way down a series of narrow passages next, he went on to delicately touching the rock wall that led into a sharp turn, half-expecting to meet a dead end, but almost immediately afterward — he was tumbling down some cave steps. His breath hitched before he landed with clumsy swerving that brought him to towering shelves of scrolls, rock tablets, and leaves with writing painted on their bodies. 'An archive?' He blinked a few times, then began craning his neck and lifting a hand to brush these things — except there were various voices nearby, some laughing, some hooting.

Rosier, slow, turned his face, shuffled a little closer to the shelves, and placed a hand on the dust-shrouded wood. Careful, he peered between two standing scrolls and saw two demons. They were standing and drinking chalices, their chuckles clouding the circular seating area among the towers of writing, their words hardly audible over the noise of skin beating against skin, low groans and cries, and high whimpers. A demon was seated on the ground, one hand holding a smoking roll of what must've been strong herbs given the room's musky earth scent, and had another horned creature settled on his lap, hips rising, then falling. His rhythm was constant, braids tossing against his back, and from his mouth — streams of pleasured gasps. For a few seconds, Rosier didn't realize it was Asmodeus sitting below, but the indistinguishable sound of his drawn-out grunts was loud over the standing demons' talk.

One said, "But the expansion will never get done at this rate. Satan has been too busy with the trials and Moloch is terrorizing everyone who lives on the southern bloc. Satan's dukes are all useless, even that asshole Baal. Asmodeus — weren't you friends with him up in Heaven? You should just ask him to give you the title—"

Asmodeus snapped, "Maybe if you got on your knees and sucked on the half of my cock that doesn't fit inside this whore, then I'll think about it."

A scorch butterflied across Rosier's cheeks as the two standing demons laughed, but the speaker indeed lowered his body, took hold of the waist of the demon on Asmodeus to still his moving. With a teasing chuckle, he brought his mouth to the front of the penetrated stranger, flicking his tongue against the untouched, quivering stiffness. The stranger let out a needing whine, then Rosier watched as Asmodeus took a hip on the one he was buried inside of and begin to rock steadily into him. Such stimulation raised the pitch of the demon-in-between's voice, and he jerked, almost violently, beneath the dual attention.

Rosier shut his eyes, inhaling through his nose, listening to the wet, mouthy noises, along with the continued slaps of bodies meeting again and again. Asmodeus had grown vocal once more, his groans dragging on as if up Rosier's spine. A hand had curled into a fist and kneaded a thigh anxiously, but Rosier had come here for this, to watch again. 'He likes it when Asmodeus is inside him. He also likes it when the other angel puts his mouth on his front.' Rosier didn't understand why, but he wanted to know. What was it *inside* that could make an angel sing? He felt his body shift, lower itself, until he was about crouching, then he opened his eyes a sliver. Now, he looked past two tilted tablets, and he better saw Asmodeus' face, the sweat dribbled on his forehead, his clenched teeth, the tight tension of his monstrous muscles. A guttural, desperate moan ripped out of him.

And Rosier's hand, shivering in fear, trailed along his thigh, not daring to look as he began to feel his own muscles coiling tighter and tighter under his skin, heating how his face had warmed up just moments ago. With his other hand, he tugged his tunic upward, exposing himself to the cold air, then flinched. This was deeply shameful, this felt wrong, but he was intent now to see if he had been mistaken that night in paradise. He wanted to understand. Would he be able to take Asmodeus' cock if he understood? 'Would I be able to make Asmodeus happy? Would I be like the other demons?' Clamping down on his bottom lip, Rosier skimmed his fingers along the side of what Asmodeus had wanted so desperately once. 'Maybe he still does.' He remembered how that other demon Asmodeus slept with had looked oddly like him.

A hand placed itself right at the rousing, the very tip, and he stroked circles. Instantly, he shuddered, but the sensation was too much like that of nausea. The shock it gave him was almost wholly unpleasant, but he tried again. He touched some more, and it felt strange, felt new. He listened to Asmodeus and the other demon fuck the one in between them, a third lover approaching with drunken amusement. "Mm." He tried a better grip, tugging on skin, molding it in his very hands, but his heart was beating faster and faster, too much. He didn't like that he felt as if he were running, nor did he like that his chest was feeling tighter. Yet, he gasped when he realized how sensitive he was here, and how his fingers were now oddly moist. What was this? He rocked against his hand, then bit down a cry. Again, a shock of something; it may have been pleasure, but he wasn't sure.

He shifted his hand, thinking of what was inside, rather than outside to be, apparently, toyed with. Rosier caught his knees shaking, and he set one down as he leaned forward, used the hand also tugging up his clothing to brace himself against the shelves. With damp fingers, he prodded at that place now, that burrow.

'You wanted this,' he thought to Asmodeus. 'You wanted it so much that you were willing to hurt me for it once.' Rosier didn't think he could accommodate his own fingers; he must've been created too closed, whereas the demon currently on top of his friend was created lovingly open and eager to invite. Flinching, Rosier pressed his index in slow, the muscle embracing him with a choking grip. It didn't feel like much at all, and worse still — it felt uncomfortable. It wasn't pleasurable, and Rosier almost went into a heated, breathless panic. "Ah." The feeling of his skin latching onto his finger was visceral, strange, and incomprehensibly bad. 'What am I doing?' He pulled out his hand, feeling warmth return to his face. 'That can't be how it's supposed to feel, is it?'

The demon on top of Asmodeus was now nearly screaming in pleasure, but a third demon soon took him by the hair and slid into the wailing mouth.

Rosier couldn't stand the sight, looking down, trying to focus entirely on the sound of Asmodeus' moans as he asked himself what he may have done wrong. His hand hadn't pleasured him much inside, and though he was filled with a fear like he'd be hit or beaten for not enjoying himself, he moved his hand to his front again because it was easier. He chewed on the inside of his cheeks, and furrowed his brow, took hold of himself again, and chased his kneading palm and fingers. Each touch brought him a tiny shock that almost felt nice, too much so — it felt like *too much* more than it felt nice at all.

When his thighs seized with a tremble that climbed all the way up to his hips, rocking them forward unwillingly — he, only barely, managed to muffle a cry by squeezing his lips together. And though he felt a sort of pulsing, needy sensation at his groin, he yanked away his hand as if were stabbed there. Clammy fingers tugged down on his tunic as Rosier realized what he'd done, *felt* it stickily; though he'd prepared for this mentally for weeks, all the imagining had turned out horribly inadequate to even a second of the pleasure-like feeling he couldn't quite call pleasure but couldn't call pain. Even more still, he hadn't anticipated this amount of hefty, crushing shame coming down on his shoulders and neck. Rosier realized his chin had lifted somewhat, lowered it; before him, he saw sin again.

'I forgot,' he told himself, 'that this is sin.' A grimace contorted his face, and every sound reaching him of slapping, of moans, of wet dribbling, and huffing made his stomach lurch in disgust. Rosier couldn't stand the sight of any of them suddenly, found them as foul as corpses half-decomposed, blooming open with insects. He saw Asmodeus' face, flushed, moaning in between his beastly growls — and in a sudden ferocious repulsion, Rosier turned away. One foot planted itself on the ground sturdy, then Rosier tried to scamper in the opposite direction, his heart battering against the front of his chest as his ribs tried to cage it tighter. He kept his head down, hurrying toward the steps. If Asmodeus or the other demons saw him, he wouldn't be able to bear it; he felt such sickness that he wondered if this was dying.

Why had he done this? Why did he ever think he was going to like it? 'Something is wrong with me. No, something is wrong with all of them.' His feet carried him faster, faster. 'They're all demons, and I'm just a fallen angel.' He felt as if he should scream, but he couldn't force it out a throat searing shut. 'I don't belong here. I should have stayed in Heaven. I never should have come here!' Rosier stepped out into the corridor, breathing in harshly to try not burst into worthless, pitiful sobs like he'd done the last time he confronted Asmodeus and his wicked lust.

"Rosier!" But that was him, his old friend.

The fallen angel of fruit staggered to a stop, almost rammed into a passing demon with a basket on his shoulder of charcoal who merely sidestepped before continuing forward. Again, he had to hunt for air to reel into his mouth, but it wasn't long before Rosier looked behind him, his face flushed now in a different kind of exertion. "Asmodeus?" He saw the dark hair of his friend in total disarray, like the tendrils of a dead octopus, cascading over his hastily tied robe. "What are you doing?"

"Did you..." Asmodeus panted, then he flinched painfully. "Did you see?" He swayed in place; one of his feet was twisted awkwardly, the stitching at the ankle drooping like a dark outline of ocean tides.

"See what?" It left Rosier's mouth softly, almost a whisper, and he blinked his muddy golden eyes.

"Rosier—" It could have been a beg, but for what?

'Who are you begging to? God? Begging Him to spare you from this? From me?' "I'm sorry." 'I'm sorry I'm in your life.' "I didn't see." He shook his head, his feet moving again. "I promise that I didn't. Whatever it was that you were doing, you don't ever have to worry about me... seeing." Rosier was trying to say that he would always look away; he didn't want to be a burden to his closest friend of millions of years. "I'm going to bed now. I'll wait for you there." He thought of Asmodeus' hands around him, Asmodeus' face resting by his nape, Asmodeus' thigh pushing between Rosier's legs; it was a position they were often in during their angel days. It had been different then. "Like always."

Asmodeus stepped forward, eyebrows curved, his gaze over-brimming with some kind of frantic terror. "Rosier, don't lie. Please don't lie to me."

"Lie?" It may have been Rosier's first sin. "I can't lie." He was an angel; everyone said it, even the devil did. "Return to what you were doing, Asmodeus." Rosier felt raw at his groin, like he'd burned himself there. "Don't worry about me." He was entirely walking away now. In Heaven, sometimes Rosier needed to sit in a dark, quiet place — not talk, not be touched — and Asmodeus had always known, not following when Rosier obviously wanted to be alone. "Goodnight." He turned and ran away properly this time, thinking of every attempt at a body for Asmodeus, every creature butchered in his name, and searched for an exit out from the caves, needing sunlight to rattle him awake from the night-mare he was living. Countless demons saw him, some snorting like those who'd seen him earlier. Their laughter was indistinguishable as he ran, their voices melting into a boiling pot that smoked and smoked until Rosier was half-blind and choking up on it all.

The sky he reached was not the one he'd been beneath with Lucifer. Blue in the shades of joy and calm were being cannibalized right before him — by reds, oranges, the flames of the sun leaking into the protective sea that cradled the world. At the same time, the color was familiar, like the firmament of the city he'd grown up in, the one up in the sky. God has a sense of humor, doesn't He? Rosier ran for the most crowded group of trees there was. To hide from his Father's daily mocking, the beautiful sunsets — the second of Heaven on Earth.

THE FIFTH MEMORY

'I almost surrendered after the eleventh body I had made for you. None were the right fit. Each one seemed worse than the last. You gargled on blood until it seeped from between your clenched teeth, and there was no hand, no leg, no chest that rose when I pressed it to you. I fear I fell into the same temptation as the devil: trying to act like God. I can only be punished for this blasphemy.' A new word. 'How many times have I asked you to forgive me, Asmodeus? How many times have I cried about how I never should have done this to you?' But sitting against the legs of the same stone table Rosier had worked tirelessly over for months, perhaps a year already, so long he'd been forced to move to a room closer to an entrance of the caves — frustration was balling in his throat. Satan himself had helped with many of the bodies, particularly the last few, always snarling at Rosier and taking his hand and trying to guide him in dismembering each creature unlucky enough to stumble upon Baal. Even still, it hadn't been enough. 'How many times have I whimpered to myself that I never should have hurt you?'

There was a new body again, one with a clawed foot and a torso patterned by stitches and different skins, and though it was one of Rosier's more angelic-shaped creations, attaching

Asmodeus' head to it had resulted in nothing more than the usual twitching, then stillness.

'But— Why did *you* hurt *me?*" Rosier's hands threaded into his too-short hair. 'Maybe you're still suffering because of what *you* did. Why did you hurt me? Why didn't you listen when I tried to push you off of me? That's not what a friend does. A friend doesn't hurt a friend. I didn't know what you were doing.' And now he was so angry that his hands trembled as they traveled toward his face. 'Maybe I shouldn't fix you. If I do, won't you just try to hurt me again? How can I know you won't? I'm trying to repair the angel I loved, but he's gone. I can't go back to who you were.' On the altar, the body stirred in place, a convulsion of its limbs that struck the air like instrument chords. 'Maybe I want you broken forever! I want to carry your decapitated, bleeding head with me for the rest of eternity. Maybe I've come to hate you more than I ever loved you!'

"*Rosier,*" — a fatal, needing groan.

The fallen angel twisted his head back at the same time his feet staggered beneath him, lifting him up in a stumble. Eyes widening to try and fit all the horror rippling onto his face, Rosier watched as a knee bent upwards, then a hand dragged along the stone before gripping it at its edge. The body turned over as it was trying to sit, and it was soon stumbling off the table in entirely, but the movement was too abrupt and stitching at the chest tore, dribbling red down his figure. 'Your voice.' Asmodeus moved from one side to another, nearly toppling with each slow step; his face was all paleness, bloodshot, desperation, and open-mouthed rasps. 'Your first word since Heaven, since what I did to you.' His name. "Asmodeus." 'Moving toward me. You're coughing up all your pain. The glow of torches is behind me — like sunlight — and your shadows make you look so much larger. You're melting into them. You're a beast.' He had made a beast. But Asmodeus tried to embrace him; his face fell into a grief-stricken dread before his heavy arms tried to come around Rosier clumsily. 'You're falling.' His weight was collapsing over him, and

Rosier's knees buckled. 'You fell, and you dragged me down, and I let you.'

They hit the floor in a thudding, painful heap. Rosier nonetheless held Asmodeus tight, feeling new warmth between the neck and shoulder where Rosier had his face nuzzled. For many minutes, they were quiet. For hours more, their laid bodies remained tangled over the ground.

And for many days, Asmodeus could hardly speak, mostly grunting and pointing, and he could not walk quite at all. He had control of his legs, but his balance was always tipped in one direction or the other, and so Rosier decided to add a tail one evening; it didn't improve his walking much, but he could at least stand upright. The new body, in fact, needed many adjustments — an entire new left arm, for example — and with each addition, it only became more monstrous, but it seemed God had decided this one was the perfect fit for him. Rosier wasn't sure of that, really — if God was involved in any of this, but it was easier to think that the Lord that'd flung them down from paradise was continuing to ruin their lives rather than having to admit this could be his own doing. No one warns you that creation carries so much guilt. And Rosier was not made for shame; he couldn't hold it; he felt that he'd collapse if he admitted his role in Asmodeus' present suffering.

There was nothing but wails of pain for a while. Rosier kept Asmodeus confined to his bed, napping in between his friend's bleeding and cries and vomit of rejected organs. He listened to the choked up sobs and the occasional shout of, "God, kill me!" when his friend chose not to suffer in silence. When it came to eating, Rosier fed Asmodeus liquids and crushed foods on the few days he could stomach it. To soothe pain, Rosier rocked him in his lap and hummed and tried to slow the rot of his body with oils. He nodded at Asmodeus' incomprehensible blubbers of tired agony, cleaned him, dressed him. It was almost instinct to do all this; it was reminiscent of how he'd looked after Lucifer during the wars on Earth. The thought that he was helping the beast that had tried to forever harm him in Heaven lingered in his mind, never disappearing but never blooming into any action either. He was not made for shame, and he was not made for anger. Anger tired him even more than tending to every wound did.

With a pair of canes that Rosier carved the ends of, Asmodeus began learning to walk again, even making a joke: "Look, Rosier, I can use these to push demons out of our way in the halls so they don't step on you." Baal visited when he could, excited to talk to his old friend again and offer him some foraged mushrooms and herbs that simmered down the aches. Other demons appeared to find Asmodeus' body fascinating, always asking to touch it, to touch him. No one seemed to mind that Asmodeus was rotting except for Asmodeus and except for Rosier. He continued mending him. He had to dress him every day; he had to feed him. Things were not well, but Asmodeus' voice filling the room was welcome, was familiar.

It was not so bad that Asmodeus was completely dependent on him; Rosier felt safer that way. Asmodeus couldn't hurt anyone as long as he was like this, even when he began wanting something of a cock. At first, he'd tried to hide this, but Rosier had once returned home to Asmodeus bleeding severely in between his legs, a shriveled organ on the ground between his animal feet, and tears in open, almost innocently terrified eyes. There was a second where Rosier truly considered denying it to him, really realized that he had the power to do it and have Asmodeus at his mercy. But pity had him walk closer, ignore Asmodeus' profuse apologizing, and begin to clean him. If Asmodeus wants it, Rosier said, then he'll make the adjustment, no matter how much his hands shook. Asmodeus whispered a choked "I love you," and Rosier kissed his forehead.

This all made Rosier feel a little better, always thinking that he could hurt Asmodeus terribly, though he had no desire to. 'I'm a good angel. An angel forgives. An angel bears it all.' But he couldn't forgive, so maybe he would try to simply not remember. Each night, Rosier hugged the rotting beast of his friend, choosing the kindness he'd been taught was the golden rule of Heaven. Love was always the right choice, wasn't it? 'I want to believe kindness and love are still true. Even in the face of something as terrible as this, all I want is to keep loving. I hope that we can one day love again like we once did.'

CHAPTER 5

With a jarring startle against grass and some kind of fabric, Rosier realized he'd been asleep, and that after he'd disappeared into the forest, he must've fallen and decided to stay over the ground to listen to all of Earth's chattering until it turned a drowsy lullaby. Arms, too, were around him, cradling him. Rosier watched a gray mist whirring over his head, not unlike when Asmodeus had first placed a rolled joint of herbs to his own groaning lips. It took several blinks, trying to do away with the unfocused dark smears over his sight, before the tall, monstrous demon was coming into view before him. It was a glow cast over Asmodeus' tired eyes, his unfamiliarly sullen features, and the sharp sound of crackling. Without daring to shift his half-lidded gaze, Rosier he knew it was fire. "Asmodeus?" His voice was hushed, small.

At the sound, Asmodeus appeared both relieved and deeply saddened with a perk of his shoulders, then a smile on his lips that didn't reach his eyes quite at all. "Oh, you didn't need to wake up," he said. "Sleep all you like. I just wanted to ensure no animal found and thought you easy prey."

'Prey.' Rosier blinked once, feeling heavy and wholly defenseless in the arms of his friend. 'I feel like prey even without any animals here.' But he heard some sharp calls from nearby, from the trees — creatures of every kind that had proliferated on the Earth to dance over the bones of numerous beasts they would never know of. "How long," came quiet, soft words from between Rosier's lips, "have I been here?" There were specs of light above, between the branches, and perhaps the hint of a thin crescent.

"Not long," was the simple answer, though there was a tinge of shame along the words. "An hour or so. I've been here with you."

Rosier's eyes fluttered shut, and he focused on his own breathing, almost forgetting how he'd gotten here or what had happened, what his hands had done, but panic didn't seize him, not like it had when he'd run away. Asmodeus' grip was gentle on him, and momentarily, he could convince him that what occurred hours ago had been a mere nightmare. Of course, he could still feel the ghost of shame between his legs, but if he tried, he could make himself forget, he could return to life as it had been when he'd simply ignore the smell of Asmodeus when he returned to bed.

"Rosier, can I ask you about what happened?"

'No,' Rosier wanted to say. 'I committed a horrible sin.' "I don't want to talk about it. I'm sorry."

Once, in Heaven, Rosier had accidentally knocked over a porcelain sculpture he'd been gifted and worked entire years decorating, turning around just in time to watch it shatter. He'd been so saddened by the loss of his labor, and that of the sculptor, that he couldn't leave his home for days and refused to eat. Angels can't starve, of course, but they can suffer. He'd wanted to suffer. When Asmodeus took notice, he'd taken Rosier's arm and wrenched him from bed. The usual aloof, disinterested voice of Asmodeus' rose to a sharp scolding; he ordered Rosier to stop mistreating himself. It was so uncharacteristic that Rosier had hurriedly done as told, trying to continue life without his precious little art piece. It was a vivid memory in an endless sea of life to remember. How does our heart choose which memories to keep? Even the mundane moments hurt, maybe they even hurt the most.

Asmodeus once again spoke with a stern edge, like he had that time in Heaven — he was ancient and he was wiser, though it was easy to forget — "Rosier, we're going to talk about this."

Cheeks warming, Rosier murmured, "Why?" He turned his head away, staring directly into the flames. "I like it better if we don't talk about it."

"It?"

"Us," left Rosier's mouth, hushed and hurt.

Sighing, rubbing a thumb on Rosier's skin in imperfect circles. "We're not in Heaven anymore." They had fallen, and they had new words lodged in their throat for what they wanted and who they were. "But—" A harsh breath escaped from Asmodeus. "It's easy to forget when I'm with you." Within Rosier's chest, his lungs stuttered. "You've never stopped being an angel to me."

Rosier had the thought that perhaps it wasn't only him that had tried to avoid a confrontation or even just a discussion, and he turned his face back to Asmodeus, slow, saw and heard the unease of the demon. He replied, "I'm sorry." He remembered his hands again, how he had touched himself, then the flood of disgust inside him. "I know I shouldn't be this way anymore."

"Don't apologize," Asmodeus answered, "I'm the one who should be asking for forgiveness. I didn't want you to see. I didn't want to frighten you. I knew that it would. After what happened. I wanted you to think that I've changed. I don't want you to be scared of me."

Curious, Rosier asked very softly, "When did you... begin?" So long, Asmodeus had needed help for everything. His groans were constant, his grunts and his bleeding. Rosier would grip him by the torso to help him practice walking circles around the room, and he'd feel the stitching along Asmodeus' belly pull dangerously beneath his fingers. Often, Asmodeus remained naked, and after the incident in which he'd butchered in between his legs, Rosier would sometimes stare at the flaccid thing he'd attached there. Something from a beast, something he could only look away from whenever it twitched.

"Earlier than you think." Rosier flinched at that but continued listening. "Even before I could walk on my own. Sometimes, you'd leave and a demon or two would come by, and they'd ask to try fucking me because my body was so horrific that they found it attractive. I liked that. I liked being wanted. And it felt good, so, so goddamn good. It even helped me forget all the pain I feel constantly. But my need to fuck was like an animal's — like my body depended on it, like I needed to claim and bite and breed or else God made me for nothing. I want to say that I wasn't like this before, but I can't be sure. I'm afraid I've always wanted this. I'm afraid I was a fuck-obsessed bastard even when you loved me so innocently in Heaven. Maybe I always wanted the need and the high, the taste and the heat, and this is what I was made for."

Each word skinned Rosier's heart greater and greater until it felt entirely raw. "I wish I could understand."

Painfully, "I do too." Asmodeus' hands trembled as they grazed up and down Rosier's arms, the touch soothing despite what he was saying. "But I also don't. I told you that you're like an angel still, and it's my own damn fault we're here. I'm the monster, and you're not. You don't deserve to be in this place: the devil's world of shit and death." Rosier didn't reply, but he lifted a hand of his own to his chest, clutching at the material of his tunic some, thinking of the cotton of his robes in paradise. "But I do. I go out and fuck a lot. I didn't want you to see, so I tried to be secretive about where I did it. And I decided not to tell you, but I should have. I shouldn't have let you find out this way. Forgive me."

After Rosier had pieced Asmodeus together for the first time and the two laid on the ground, Asmodeus had uttered his second and third words since the decapitation: "*Forgive me.*" A gasping, hoarse pleading as Asmodeus choked up on blood. Then, he'd said his name again. Rosier, Rosier, Rosier.

"I already knew," Rosier answered, partly ashamed, enough to want to bury his face in his friend's chest. "I was trying to make peace with it." He stared into Asmodeus' eyes, as dark as the abyss above. "With you... doing that." 'After what you did to me.' "I think I'll have to keep searching for peace, but you can walk on your own now. You can do as you wish."

Asmodeus's next question was more direct: "Do you want me to find another place to sleep?"

Instantly, Rosier jolted, finally rising to sit up before Asmodeus with his body aching like a bruise. "Hm?" He hated it, hated those words, but he couldn't decipher why they hurt him. "No. I don't want that." He shook his head. "I need to help in case anything tears or hurts during the night." Rosier was thinking of the night he curled around Asmodeus' head on the first mattress he'd been able to lay on since Heaven, the feathers stuffed in the cloth feeling like a cruel joke of his own once heavy but wonderful wings. "I need to..." 'Take care of you.'

Lowly, Asmodeus replied, "I can take care of myself well enough now."

Rosier's eyes itched; he wanted to say, 'I don't know how to stop caring for you.' "But—" A breath tumbled out, and he had no clue what direction to take his words. Should he say that couldn't continue living without Asmodeus to care for? Should he say that he would be cold every night if he had to return to sleeping alone? "I like you." It was such an obvious statement, and yet it felt like a confession. "And I... like sharing a bed." Asmodeus parted his lips, but Rosier added, "It makes me happy." 'You make me happy.' Then, Asmodeus' eyes were terribly soft.

"I don't share beds with other demons," he said. "I'm not sure that I want to."

Rosier murmured, "Then we should stay together."

Though his mouth was pressed thin, Asmodeus' face flickered with relief. "I'm happy you think that." Something nearby rattled menacingly.

"I ask that you don't," Rosier said, "tell me too much about what you do." He laid his hands on the damp grass, then pushed up his body, wanting to return to the cave. "I hope you understand."

"Of course. Of course." Then, quieter — "Rosier?"

"Yes?" Rosier turned his head as he was halfway standing, and he caught Asmodeus beside him, already on his feet, leaning to peck his lips. A kiss — simple, chaste, almost amicable.

Against him, his beloved friend whispered, "Thank you."

"What for?" Rosier stared at Asmodeus' mouth, wondering if other demons had it whenever they liked, if Asmodeus laid those lips to suck every demon that begged for it.

"Not despising me after what I've done."

Rosier frowned a little, wanting to say that he wasn't sure that he didn't. Instead, he turned his head up to Asmodeus, reached for his hands, felt his fingers brush the talons of an animal that he'd attached to Asmodeus in the absence of any creature with opposable thumbs. "We should return. I'm hungry." He kissed Asmodeus on the mouth again, innocent and soft, and he felt his friend squeeze his hand gently back. 'I wish I could understand. I wish I enjoyed what I did to my body earlier. But sometimes I wish you'd just never done that to me. Never hurt me the way that you did.'

After killing the bonfire, the two demons walked hand in hand toward the caves. 'I think I am angry. I think I'm frustrated. It's only clearer now that I'm not like you or any of the other demons.' Asmodeus nuzzled his hair with his nose. 'I wish I could stop feeling chained by my memories. Sometimes, all I can do is think of what's happened. All I can do is think about you pressing me onto the bed, then taking my legs, the empty look in your eyes. I wish we could both forget, but we can't. And if we can't hold the innocence of before, then I just wish to learn to be happy here. I'll learn to be happy with you doing with other demons what you wanted to do with me.' Rosier wanted another kiss, and he received it. 'And I think you'll learn to be happy pretending the bodies you touch are mine.'

"One day, when you were carrying me," said Asmodeus, "Satan told all the dukes that Michael was a coward. A betrayer. You weren't paying attention, but I was. He said that none of us would have suffered if it weren't for Michael being too afraid to face our Father. His fear of God eclipsed his love." He allowed that to linger. "I always did think Michael was a fraud. Angel of God-given strength but none of his own. And I hardly pity Lucifer, but he was right about Michael and about God. It was all so fucking perverted in end, wasn't it? Heaven? Maybe this place is no better, but at least I don't need God's blessing to love you anymore."

CHAPTER 6

Baal was laughing. "Rosier, none of the demons are going to take you seriously."

In the midst of tucking a flower by his ear, the fallen angel blinked curiously at his reflection — the fluttering image on the surface of a bowl of water settled between his thighs as he sat on the floor. "Mm?" He lifted his chin to see Baal, leaning against the closed doorway. "Why do you say that?" As he spoke, a petal — stark white from a lily — stumbled down from his hair, landed softly by one of his sandals. "Oh," he breathed, then reached for it.

Instead of replying, Baal turned his snicker to Asmodeus. "Should I tell him or should you?"

Asmodeus merely grunted; he was on the floor with Rosier but lying on his back with an entire left arm severed to the shoulder. With his right hand, he was shoveling fistfuls of mushroom into his mouth from a leaf serving as a plate. He chewed loud and ground his teeth before replying, "How about you make yourself useful and find me something to snort, instead? I need something stronger if this pain won't do the favor of killing me." Beige bandages over the stump where his arm ended were deep red, would need to be replaced soon; his left shin, as well, had taken on a severe green undertone, some decayed dark already patching along the surface like boils on water, and it was the most concerning at the ankle, where one might catch an insect trying to burrow. According to Asmodeus, it had become too painful to stand recently.

"I'll look for something," Baal promised. "But before I forget, Ishtar told me he wanted to fuck you this morning. Do you think that'd help at all? We can share him." Rosier immediately frowned, finally lowering his hands from the flowers in his hair, turning away from his reflection but not looking to either of the demons in the room with him.

Asmodeus replied, "You'll have to carry me to wherever he is."

"It shouldn't be far."

"Then yes, but have him bring me something to snort."

Slow, the fallen angel of fruit exhaled through his nose, then saw Baal's feet step right beside him. Tilting his head upward, he met the burly duke's face again, looking down at him with a snicker still along his mouth. "You could join too, if you'd like. We could make it an orgy." Before he could stop himself, Rosier imagined a dozen or so bodies against each other, dampened by all sorts of fluids, their claws grazing, their tails curling around limbs, and a deep grimace drowned his face. "What?"

Asmodeus spoke again: "Rosier has something else to do tonight. Don't bother. Now, stop wasting time and head to the court before the devil gets impatient."

Rosier nodded, climbing to his feet. "Yes—" His voice trembled, and he looked to Asmodeus, wanting to thank him, but Asmodeus' eyes were shut. "We should head to the court, Baal. Who was it that's standing trial? Moloch?" He shuffled toward the door, tugging down on his tunic, then balling his hands in the long cloak that hung down from his shoulders. "And we're certain Lucifer said I *must* go?"

Hesitantly, Baal nodded, as well, then turned to lead the way out, gesturing vaguely. "Yes, it's Moloch, and Lucifer told me to remind you that you have no choice in attending." As they stepped through the door, Rosier's gaze flickered again to Asmodeus. "He didn't sound too happy when he said that. I suppose I should warn you."

"Well," Rosier whispered, "it's been months now of him trying to have me grow fruits." It was difficult to believe, but yes, months. Months, too, since Asmodeus and Rosier had spoken in the forest, discussing what they ought to do about each other. "There hasn't been... much progress." The hallways met him coolly, as did the demons peppered upon it, some sitting, some chattering, two with their lips brawling as they embraced against the wall, though not so sexually. Perhaps, a pair merely happy to see each other. 'Oh,' Rosier thought, 'I should have kissed Asmodeus before I left.'

Asmodeus' current state of rot did, at least, keep him in place; he hadn't wandered out by himself for three mornings. It shamed Rosier to be happy about it, but he was. Each time he tended to Asmodeus, he had to bite down a sigh in relief that his friend wasn't going off to sleep with four, five demons a day.

"*You*," Baal snarled at some passerby. "Don't make me have to rip off that stupid fucking tail of yours. Go back to work on the west entrance."

Four or five was Rosier's small estimate. Of course, Asmodeus' sexual habits were more of a mystery to him now that he refused to go looking for it, but he had sat in lounges with Asmodeus or eaten with him in the kitchens, heard each reference to it no matter how much he wanted to cover his ears: "Good work yesterday with those three demons sucking your cock, Asmodeus," or "Next time invite me and my friend here," and, "We heard from Gemory that you can go for hours. Mind if I see if that's true tonight, darling?" Asmodeus always returned to him washed up, but now Rosier wondered if it was any one of his partners that cleaned his body with slow, adoring hands. Did Asmodeus ever smile at them fondly?

Only twice since the incident in the archives had Rosier caught Asmodeus in the middle of the act. The first time, he'd been passing by a room only to hear demons laughing, then turned his face to see some snorting ground leaves, while Asmodeus fucked a large demon in the corner. Rosier had hurriedly left before he was noticed, but the second time, he had headed down toward the small underground lake of the mountain, where some washed, though it was much more popular to bathe out in the rivers and streams on the Earth's surface.

It was a beautiful place — the rocks a copper color, long stalactites hanging overhead, dripping onto some of the two or three dozen heads of demons. The smell here, too, was quite different from anywhere else on the mountain — more earthy and brisk and fresh. Rosier didn't often come to the subterranean waters, precisely because they were often populated with a few demons fornicating along the rim of crystalline, bright blue. But Rosier had been curious to try bathing here, now that he'd grown so skilled at looking the other way from sex, but there were some snickers from someone, then a demon coming up behind Rosier, huskily saying into his ear that he could help wash his soft, angelic body. Instantly, Rosier had jolted away and stumbled aside, nearly slipping, until he'd heard another voice and turned his head to it.

Asmodeus was pulling his dripping mouth away from a demon, claws still planted on his thighs, then snapped at the one harassing Rosier to find someone else to fuck. When Asmodeus' eyes trailed back to Rosier, they held a gleam of regret. Rosier had turned on his heel without a word and headed for the way he'd come in, hearing demons snicker at him while one groaned at Asmodeus for ruining their fun. Another asked why he seemed to like Rosier so much. Rosier had desperately wanted to say, 'We're friends, that's why. We've been friends for eternity. None of you would understand, would you?! None of you know what a friend is anymore.' But he knew that wasn't true.

"Rosier," Baal said, "I've been curious about something." And Rosier made an affirming hum, allowing him to continue. "I've never seen you at an orgy. Do you only fuck Asmodeus?"

Slowly, Rosier breathed in. "I don't..." He shook his head. "I don't fornicate with him."

"What? Are you joking?"

"I don't have much of an interest in that, Baal."

"Oh. You're a virgin?" Baal laughed. "Well, you'll feel differently once you start doing it. You should ask Asmodeus to help you."

Rosier bit the inside of his cheeks before focusing on the path ahead. He should focus. He should ignore Baal; he should stop thinking about his relationship with Asmodeus for one second. He was a duke. 'I don't want to be.' But he was, and he'd have to listen to the trial and offer his opinion to Lucifer.

Already, he could see the gaping hole in the cave that led into the throne room like a great maul; at either side, there were two demons with iron swords that had some reddened rust along the edges of the blades. Surely, they were remnants from the wars before Satan's resurrection. Just as Baal descended onto the first step leading to the theater, then continued climbing downward, he shouted at some demons, telling a few others to settle, then yelling at some faraway dukes to get onto the stage with their king. Rosier looked to either side of him to see the blabbering audience, perhaps two hundred, on the many seats in a half-circle before the throne — which was a great wooden seat on a high platform with tusks at its crown and adorned with several more beast skeletons. There were five dukes disorganized at Satan's reach while the devil sat in his chair regally, wearing a robe of furs and all of his jewelry, much of which had been gifted to him at his funeral.

Lucifer, too, wore a crown of thorns and bone as he lifted his chin, saw Baal and Rosier, and looked quite prepared to spit at them for taking so long, but he said nothing. Instead, he waved for his princes to divide evenly at either side of him, this gesture also seeming to quiet the crowd and to make a muscular, short-haired demon step into the court's center with his arms crossed — Moloch. Rosier tried not to look at him as he walked past, then headed for Lucifer's left while Baal went for the right. He found himself fiddling with his cloak again and, in the process, noticed that he seemed a little overdressed for the demons nearby in simple tunics or open robes. They had no flowers in their hair; horns, instead.

Many demons in the crowd had horns. Why?

"Silence," Lucifer called, not shouting, though many reacted as if he had: the crowd startled and hurried to sit. Then, he crossed his legs and leaned back into his seat, tilting his head curiously at the center of the court. "Moloch," Satan greeted. "I hate to see you here again."

"Pure shit from your mouth at times, Lucifer," the demon grumbled, and Rosier instantly drew a breath. "You've already decided, haven't you? How about we don't bother arguing and move onto the punishment?"

"Punishment for what?" Satan asked, so amicably it was almost believable. "What did you do, duke?"

"Stop fucking around with me," spat the demon back.

"I can't punish you if I don't know what you did, but you seem to think you deserve suffering." Taking a strand of golden hair between two fingers then twirling it mindlessly, the devil went on, "And, I should say, if you're so sure you should be punished, then why did you ever do it?"

Furrowing his brow, Moloch hesitated, but soon scoffed, laughed so heartily that his shoulders shook, turned back to the audience like this were all a great joke and he expected everyone to be cackling along with him. "Oh," he was saying, "I could ask you the same question, couldn't I? Why commit any sin at all? You were the one that taught this to us, Satan. I did it because it felt good. You taught me that — *pleasure*. You never said there were rules on how to please ourselves. I thought sin was about freedom."

"I taught you fucking," Satan answered calmly. "But rape is a torture. If I allowed such rampant rape within these caves, then I might as well allow for war. When I gathered you all, I said that God laughs at our chaos, that He uses our violence as proof to the angels that we cannot rule ourselves, so when I order you to control your sin, I do it for the purpose of unity — not out of some moral high ground. Consider yourself to be in contract to every other demon that lives on the Earth. You should commit only the violence you're willing to face for yourself."

"What does it matter," Moloch grumbled, "what God thinks or what the angels think? I didn't fall for a love of *unity*. I fell because I wanted *more*." 'More pleasure than God offered us to have in Heaven,' Rosier thought sadly. "Not because I wanted to be on our best behavior for God on Earth!"

The devil said, "Do you think this is a godless place?" The duke Moloch's jaw visibly clenched. "You think you abandoned God to worship your own sin?" Then, Moloch was parting his mouth, frustrated eyes screwing shut for a fraction of a second. "*You fell,*" Satan seethed, "*to worship me.*" At this, Moloch sighed roughly, and Lucifer rose to stand, nose turned up. "Is this how you speak to your god, Moloch?" He stepped, the tap of his bare foot echoing in the dense silence of the room. "A duke who doesn't respect his king can't be a duke."

"I don't see," Moloch hissed, but not daring face Lucifer now, "the *purpose* of this, the purpose of this peace you want to maintain."

"Don't forget that were it not for me, you'd still be in Heaven unable to fuck, unable to be free. Should I deliver you back to the God above if you won't worship the one before you?" Satan took another few steps forward, dangerously approaching the way down into the space where Moloch stood. "Have you forgotten what I did for you? Sacrificed for you? God's favorite angel gave up paradise to lead you all to freedom, and you disrespect it all?"

Only as he'd reached the edge of the stage did Rosier notice that Lucifer had, tucked into his filigree golden belt, an earthly brown leather whip with a rather short base and multiple tails with knotted ends. "You would be *nothing* without me."

"But what's the *purpose* of this all, Lucifer?!" Moloch answered with a touch of desperation, looking at him now with wider eyes. How could he dismiss the beautiful messiah who had shown him the extents of violence and pleasure? How could a demon be so disrespectful toward his own creator — Satan?

"You see no purpose in defying God?" Satan asked, but his voice had grown calmer, more soothing. His hand curled around the end of his whip, and Rosier's body tensed as he caught specs of red on the dirt by Moloch's feet.

"Soon," Moloch replied, "we're all going to burn, aren't we?" Burn? Rosier blinked. "Didn't God say that we would all eat dust and suffer for what we've done? Aren't we all to be destroyed?" Rosier glanced at Baal, whose lips were pressed into a tight, thin line, then at Lucifer, whose face was stone. 'We're all going to burn?' His hands found each other, nervous, and he frowned deeply, lowering his gaze to his feet. '*Burn*?' He'd already known this, known about their coming death — theoretically, as we all do. But it felt heavier suddenly, more real than it'd ever had. "If we're all going to burn, what's the point of living well? All we can do is fuck and try to feel good before it's all over."

'Will everyone here all burn?' He didn't want to burn. He didn't want to feel the scorch of damnation ever again. He didn't want to be destroyed either.

"That's precisely why you should control yourself," Satan answered. "We no longer have eternity, so we all ought to enjoy ourselves until the end." He turned his head, but he faced no one, his gaze held on a rock wall. "From today onward, you will no longer be a duke, Moloch." Moloch didn't seem to be surprised. "And you will rot away at hard labor for thirty years but only after Baal flogs you for as long as he chooses." In an instant, Rosier heard the grunt behind him, so clear that he was yanked out from the building panic in his heart and saw his large-horned friend stalk forward, coming up behind Satan. Stealthily, the duke took the handle of Lucifer's whip and pulled it from his belt, then moved before the devil protectively; to the audience, it must've seemed like Baal had been the one who brought the weapon. He approached Moloch, whose face was twitching indignation along his mouth, his eyes.

"No," Moloch blurted, but his voice was hollow. "Fuck you, Baal. Don't you dare touch me! Bastard!"

Rosier felt his shaking fingers graze his lips, only then realizing he'd lifted a hand in fright. 'No,' he almost echoed, but he couldn't do anything but jerk his head away just as Baal lifted the whip. Not looking didn't save him from hearing the bloodcurdling howl and the sharp crack of the weapon making contact. There was a growl, then a responding one, before Baal yelled for some dukes to hold Moloch down, but Rosier's feet were rooted where they were, his very heart stopped. "No," he said aloud this time, but so quiet no one would hear over the clamor of two or three dukes running over, then another screech of the whip. Distantly, there were some hollers of joy and laughing jeers, telling Moloch to suffer. 'Burn,' continued to echo in Rosier's head.

He didn't want to burn. He didn't want these screams in his ears either. The Judgment of the rebel angels had been so long ago, and he had hardly been there, in some corner of the battle, his eyes shut so that he did not see his Father in the most shameful moment of his life. He had shouted out to be thrown from Heaven once Lucifer had been made to fall, his hearing muffled then, as it was now. But he didn't want this now, didn't want to be here. '*God, I don't want to burn. Father. Are you listening?*'

A presence came closer, a scent of lavender and metal almost as heavy as the sensation of seductive calm that washed over him. Rosier felt cold, sharp fingers touch his veins just as he heard the squelch of something ripping open and a throatier, deeper scream. Elegant, Lucifer was moving his face into Rosier's line of sight in all its gorgeous, empty smile and squint — all the beauty that even he couldn't accustom to. It mattered little that it was a mere forgery of what it had been in Heaven. "Lucifer," left his dry mouth.

"Come with me," whispered the devil to the fallen fruit angel. All around them, the demons were rising from their seats, some to cheer and others to hurry out; for once, Rosier supposed he could perfectly understand the other fallen. The frown on his face was so deep that Rosier was certain it may dig itself permanently onto his mouth as Satan tugged on him some more. "Let's go to the flowers."

Rosier stared, eyes tired. "I don't—" He shuddered when Moloch screamed again, the sound of his body thrashing in the hold of others making Rosier accidentally glance over, then shut his mouth and feel himself lurch forward in disgust. "Lucifer, I can't be here. I can't—" He wanted to return to his room. He didn't want to see Moloch's gut torn open, piles of meat breathing vibrant on the ground. Rosier wanted to return to Asmodeus, to lay with him, smother his thinking by pressing his face to the older demon's chest, maybe shut his eyes and breathe in the sweat of his rotting body.

"Then come with me to the flowers," said Satan. "Or stay here and help the others torture Moloch."

Returning to Asmodeus and curling up against him wasn't possible, regardless of his fantasies; Baal and him had planned to go fuck a demon. Rosier should leave them to it. "As you wish." Satan tugged on his wrist, but then removed his touch, turning on his heel, heading for the steps down into Moloch's torture chamber. Carefully, Rosier's foot lifted, set itself down — one step, then another. He didn't want to try and make fruits sprout, but Satan hadn't asked, he'd ordered, and Rosier was not going to argue or complain.

Together, they made their way off the stage, Satan placing his free hand on Rosier's forearm and pulling Rosier a little closer to his side. The touch was gentle, deceptively so. They made their way around Moloch as he continued crying out in pain, Rosier staring only at his sandals and narrowly avoiding stepping on a flowing river of red headed towards him. Some demons looked at their king and his pathetic duke, and most immediately bowed their heads at Satan with utter reverence but, in the process, appeared to be bowing to Rosier as well. He didn't like that.

"Friend," Satan called just as they'd climbed most of the steps toward the exit into the regular tunnels of the cave system. "I'm happy you came to the trial. It didn't look like you wanted to come when I told you to." That had been a few days ago. "What did you think of it?"

"I didn't," Rosier answered uncertainly, "think much about it." He watched those ahead of them step out of their way, allow the two to walk through the massive entrance without obstruction.

"At times, I make decisions that are unjust, you see. I chose power and control over fairness." He tilted his head at Rosier, eyes oddly reflective as always, like there was no soul behind them and Rosier could only see his own. 'But, of course, I have no soul anymore.' "Have you ever felt the same?"

"No," Rosier whispered, a foot stumbling beneath him as they stepped into the corridor, but before he could struggle to try to regain his balance, Lucifer gripped him tighter and forced Rosier to still.

"Hm." Lucifer gave him a tight-lipped smile. "You see," and he began tugging him along again, "being God, or like God, is about doing the wrong thing when it benefits you. Maybe I should also have Moloch quartered for what he's done, for raping... oh, I think it was ten this week. It's what he deserves — that I am very sure of. But some would find that disproportion-ate. He would grow resentful, and his friends would as well. Baal told me that Moloch led an army during the wars on Earth. It was a small one, but he led them nonetheless. I won't tolerate any rebellion among the demons. They're my children. They must listen to me."

Rosier parted his lips, furrowed his brow, wanting to say, 'Lucifer, you're beginning to sound like God.'

But Satan was still grinning widely, and he gave his arm another squeeze. "I know what you're thinking, Rosier — but to rule, there are some things that are non-negotiable. And aren't I more benevolent? I offer demons so much more freedom, and I only punish those who damage others and our home so excessively that the peace is corrupted."

Rosier stared at the hallway, emptier than it often was, too quiet, then answered in a small voice, "Though we'll all burn one day."

"You heard me on the throne, didn't you? We all ought to be happy before the fires begin to burn." When Rosier breathed shakily, he added, "I really am glad you came. The dread will do you some good. I want you to be happier, Rosier. I want us to grow orchards together on the Earth. I fear you're afraid to let go of the Heaven that has already abandoned you." He was telling Rosier to fall, again. "Mm, but you look so upset. I'll stop discussing this."

"Thank you," Rosier murmured, so weakly he doubted the devil had heard him.

"The solstice is in just a few weeks. I hope they'll be fruit there, but if not, there's always the next solstice." The solstice festival — Rosier had forgotten all about it. "You should take some time to rest before it comes. It'll be very fun. I hope you try to enjoy yourself." Lucifer leaned to press a kiss to the fallen angel of fruit's cheek, and Rosier shut his eyes for a moment, leaning into the lips of his friend. And though they arrived at the meadow for Rosier to once again bear no fruit — the two laid together over the flowers for some time, watching the clouds, feeling the warmth of the sun on their faces. The heat of a new season, a quarter of the clockwork that made up the Earth.

Then, some days passed.

Rosier found that he couldn't quite return to how life had been leading up to the trial for Moloch. He sat on his bed, bundled in a blanket, fingers busy with embroidering, staring at the lit fireplace and each dancing flame. Whenever Asmodeus returned, Rosier always smiled at him as kindly as he could muster. And when his older friend limped over to him, leaning on a cane or two, Rosier took his robe, tugged him down. He sighed against his mouth, then enjoyed when Asmodeus answered by devouring him in kisses. It was the only solace he could find from a persistent sadness in Rosier's heart. Lucifer had been right to call it *dread*. This overbearing, constant fear of tomorrow or the one after that. It was only Asmodeus' affection that could do away with it, even if just for a moment; he'd always clutch Asmodeus' clothes a little tighter, wanting to be closer to him than an embrace allowed.

"Asmodeus?" Rosier called one afternoon, wiping dried blood from over a new pair of stitches with a damp cloth — examining the new arm he'd painstakingly just spent hours attaching to Asmodeus' shoulder, almost the size of the other one; he'd become a lot better skilled at maintaining the beastly body's symmetry. He was better at creating now.

"Mm?" Asmodeus replied, his voice strained around the smoking roll of herbs between his lips. He turned his head to Rosier, who knelt at his side. "May I be of service, darling Rosier?" His humor was noticeably forced, his face in such a deep cringe that all his handsome features were suffocating beneath it; 'his pain must be too much.'

Frowning, Rosier said, "Maybe I shouldn't bring this up now. After you're done smoking, you should rest. I'll make some broth and get you something to drink."

"Pain's too strong to let me sleep," Asmodeus grunted, lifting his healthier arm to remove the joint in his mouth for a second, then breathe out some smoke from the corner of it, careful for none of the gray to lap at Rosier's face. "Want a taste?"

Rosier never liked smoking — the mist it rose to his head was always more disorienting than he thought he could ever care for — but he inched his face closer, and he allowed Asmodeus to press the roll to his lips. A crackling, deep drag, then the fallen angel of fruit exhaled the earthly burn. "Ah." There was no instant reaction from his body, no sign that he was doing good or that he was sinning; somehow, that was more frightening. He had no direction to turn; he was lost in a sea of feeling. "Thank you." Asmodeus chuckled as Rosier leaned in to take another drag.

"You're lovely," Asmodeus told him. "Have as much as you like."

Cheeks nicely warmed, the fallen angel of fruit whispered, "You're lovely too."

"Sometimes," came a hazy, snickering reply, "I wish it would all end. All this pain. I wish I could die." His laugh grew but not in volume — instead, it drawled longer and longer. "But I don't want to leave you. If I died, then I wouldn't be able to hold you." Asmodeus inched his hand away, tapped the end of the joint to send specs of ash onto the ground, before stubbing the lit end of the roll against the stone. "I hope you can forgive me for being so selfish."

The grass stench of the room was horribly dense, Rosier realized, but he didn't mind it. He pressed a kiss to Asmodeus' jaw, his gaze flickering down to that horrible arm of a mammal that he'd disfigured. "Aren't you scared that we will die one day in the future? That God will burn us all, then kill us?"

Asmodeus was too high; his smile was giddy and his chuckle was pitched sharper than it often was. "I've lived a long time, Rosier. Everything has to come to an end eventually. As long as I can spend these last years with you, then I can't complain." Leaving his blunt on the ground, he brushed some of Rosier's messy bangs away from his face. "But I don't think you'll burn. You're still an angel. I'm a corrupt monster that likes to fuck and kill, but you're an angel. You'll return to Heaven, one day. I'm sure."

Sadly, Rosier leaned to kiss Asmodeus on the mouth, gently,

weakly. He screwed his eyes shut, the weight of dread on his heart tugging him downward to curl up against Asmodeus by the fire. "I love you," came his whisper, throat beginning to burn, eyes itchy like scars.

"I love you too, Rosier."

"I don't want you to die."

"Don't think of it."

"I love you, I love you." The echoing of his own words was almost frantic, like clinging to a rope above the flames, like he could only root himself to where he was with that promise. "I love you so much, Asmodeus." But it was not enough; he choked up on his fear, feeling cries tear themselves out from his heart, turning wet at his eyes, dribbling down. "I don't want to lose you." Even after what occurred during the war for Heaven, Rosier hadn't been able to part ways with Asmodeus. Asmodeus who hurt him. Asmodeus who had to be taken care of by him forever until the end.

"Don't cry." Asmodeus' voice finally took on a more serious tinge, turning softer, soothing. "Rosier, please." His better arm went around Rosier before he nuzzled his head, pecking it, whispering that he was here with him, that he hadn't lost him. The words were almost embarrassing to hear; they made Rosier feel exceptionally young.

"I'm sorry," Rosier said, shaking his head. "I didn't mean to become sad like that without warning. You're in pain, and I'm the one who is selfish." Asmodeus said it was alright as the fallen angel of fruit tried to rub his eyes of the tears quickly. "I want to talk about happier things." Lucifer had said all the demons ought to enjoy themselves before the end. Perhaps that was the true difference between God and Satan: they both offered death to sinners — but one allowed them to dance their way there. "The solstice is soon... Lucifer wants to host a festival. He says it'll be a lot of fun for everyone." He brought a smile back to his face, uncertain but not untruthful. "I want to make you some clothes for that day. I want to celebrate."

"Let me make you some jewelry," Asmodeus said. "I still remember how to do it from when I learned in Heaven, and I'll help you with the clothes too."

His tiny smile grew a little, and Rosier cuddled up against his friend more. "After I bring you something to eat."

"We should both eat, but for now smoke. It'll make you feel better."

THE SIXTH MEMORY

After a few centuries of living in the caves, Baal informed Rosier that he'd finally fucked Lucifer. It was even better than the last time, their first time. Baal knew what to do now. He could take the devil's legs and kiss up from ankle to thigh, to where he could pucker his lips and suckle without guidance. Satan had been quiet, initially, but then his commands grew into hisses. His pleasured cries had him thrashing and arching against the bed, digging into it like a dagger on skin to make the mattress bleed around them. Then, he'd pulled Baal down, into the sea, like a siren, like flood, and he'd gnawed at him before they'd begun to throw bites at each other. For too long, there was no penetration, just mere arousal scraping against each other. Two tulips pecking in a kiss. Then, Satan had allowed Baal inside him, though not without wrestling the burlier demon down first. A king stabbing himself onto his duke, a mere instrument to his pleasure and nothing more. And it was several hours that passed of their bodies meeting, again and again. Barren wetness spilled and splattered to drip like dew onto the sheets. Their names were moaned against lips pressed so close together they could forget there might be yet another name in between them. Baal wouldn't mind it. Even if Lucifer cried out the name of God's angel, it would be Baal who held that beautiful body, and his grasp on those perfect hips was stronger than the ghost of the chief prince's touch.

Afterward, Satan threw Baal out of his chambers, and it would be another many centuries before he allowed Baal to share his bed to sleep. But Baal — Rosier thought — had proven to the god of the demons his loyalty. Baal would stand by Satan unconditionally, even without the promise of sex. Maybe Lucifer would learn to be satisfied with him, too, in time. We all ought to learn to be satisfied with what we have in this short life.

CHAPTER 7

osier didn't know what a festival would, or could, entail. In the days before the event, he managed to build up the courage to ask a few demons, but their answers amounted to shrugs and dismissive hand waves. There had been many great celebrations in Heaven, particularly for when a newborn arrived, which was all any demon could use as a point of reference — but as an angel, Rosier had never enjoyed the parties much. They were too loud, involved too much dancing — not that he minded dancing, especially if it was with his friend Asmodeus, but doing it in a crowd wasn't so pleasant — and went on far too long. Hence, he'd usually draw the curtains, then crawl beneath the covers in bed to muffle the songs and shouting from outside.

Asmodeus, of course, had loved the parties, though he didn't mind that Rosier didn't. Running in between the festivities and home, he'd always bring a plate of food still steaming and a drink, then take a moment to eat with Rosier. The both of them had alcohol frequently in Heaven, though only Asmodeus had developed something of a dependency on it for a few short centuries, and then again another couple centuries later — constantly asking for it, constantly vocalizing the dread to Rosier of having to be aware of where he was.

'How can,' Rosier had asked, 'you not like feeling like yourself?' 'It's not that. It's not that, brother.' 'Then?' 'It's the feeling of things, in and out of me. It exhausts me, sometimes. When you're as old as I am, you might understand, but I hope that you never do.' 'Hm, well, whenever you feel like that, tell me. I can try to help.' 'You're too good to me, brother. I don't want you to think you have to look after me all the time.' 'I like caring for you.'

If nothing else, Rosier hoped this solstice would be a good excuse to drink.

"Hey, you! Fruit demon!"

The fallen angel stopped, turned his head, which was adorned with some ribbons. He'd been yearning to interweave colorful cloth into long braids, but his hair was too short, chopped forever by his own hand. 'Maybe, while Asmodeus sleeps tonight, I'll braid a little color into his hair.' The thought almost made him smile as a tall, blonde demon sauntered over to him. 'I wonder what his lovers would think.' He blinked, steadied his vision, and saw that the demon wore an excess amount of paint on his face — a rub of pale red on his cheekbones, as well as a dust of pink by his eyes, and a ruby color draped on his lips for good measure. "Yes?" He couldn't help but think of Azazel, an old friend who'd painted his body in Heaven. 'I hope you're well, Azazel.'

"Hm." This demon's brows were furrowed, though he was quite attractive, even with horns and a swishing tail. "The dukes are looking for you. There's a room that was cleared out down the hall, toward your left. It's the largest one." He paused, then chuckled. "I thought I wouldn't find you, Rosier, but you're one of the only demons without horns in the caves."

"Oh." Rosier nodded slowly, then tried a small smile. "I see, thank you for telling me. I'll go on ahead to speak with the other dukes." But he found himself hesitating the way this demon also had, then he added, "I really don't understand why so many demons have horns now."

"Ha! Well, for me, darling," replied the demon, tapping his chest with long nails, "I kept falling over. God's cruel joke, I'm sure, but my balance stayed up in Heaven. I thought the horns would help, and they did, and so did the tail. Some other demons are like this, but really, they just look good. We're Earth creatures now, might as well look it, right?"

"Right," Rosier said, unsure.

"I think you'd look good," said the demon, "with horns.... Maybe some hooves." Then, he grinned widely. "It's Gemory."

"Oh!" The fallen angel of fruit jumped, flushing. "I didn't recognize you with the face paint..." He didn't mean for his voice to trail, but Gemory snickered at him before tapping his nose teasingly. "I should go now. Good luck with the dukes, duke." With a toss of his hair, he sauntered away, leaving Rosier to watch Gemory leave curiously. 'He seems much happier now that Moloch has been punished.' Rosier yanked at one of the two small strings at the collar of his lily-white tunic, partly hidden by the embroidered robe he wore over it.

As he thought of Gemory, Rosier also landed on the memory of having to relay Satan's order for Baal to collect animal carcasses for the demons to modify themselves with. He took the first steps in the direction that Gemory had pointed him to, wondering now why Lucifer was so adamant for demons to alter themselves. The freedom of the body seemed to matter to Lucifer more than anything. And Rosier wasn't opposed to that, per se, but too much freedom was paralyzing. If he could do anything at all to himself, then how could he choose where to cut or stitch? He liked his body, too, or he'd always thought he did.

Hurrying demons were bumping into both sides of him, almost all dressed in similar styles as Rosier, which did at least bring some relief from the constant nudity in the caves, but he chose to refrain from being grateful to Lucifer for now. He followed the directions to where the other dukes were — a wide opening into a hall, as Gemory had specified, with some flowers and colorful streamers lining the entrance. Few were passing through it with another few waiting right outside, peering in excitedly as they flapped at their painted faces with feather hand-held fans, perhaps waiting for permission to enter. They glanced at Rosier as he moved past but said nothing, and he found himself looking up at the gaps in the rock ceiling where light, and some bright green vines, dribbled onto the plush cushions on the floor, the carpets, and still-empty tables. The walls were painted with animals, plants, and sin. And, too, there were some stone steps that led upwards to a wooden throne clouded with precious stones and a wide array of flowers but nonetheless not as ornate as Satan's throne in the courtroom.

The dukes were at the center, discussing something about expansion and Moloch's angry friends. "But," Baal was groaning and settling back to lean against the edge of a stone table, "what does it matter? If they miss him, they can join him in hollowing out the way to the pools." One of the other dukes laughed and said that, soon, some demons were going to turn their anger to Lucifer. "They should know better than that. Oh— Rosier." At the name, all the dukes turned and looked at the fallen angel of fruit in question, some amused, some quirking a brow or sighing irritably. "You can leave. Gemory must've misunderstood us."

Immediately, Rosier stopped, but he'd already reached them. "Oh. I'm sorry—"

"Before you go," interjected a demon, "where's Asmodeus? We've hardly seen him."

Rosier swallowed. "He should be in bed still, but he's been feeling great these past few weeks, and he was excited to come by."

Another one of the demons jokingly cheered, and the others laughed, before he said, "Let him know he can come by early. I wanted to ask him about how to keep the east side from collapsing; it's really starting to creak. Oh and I want to see this cock I keep hearing about." Again, cackles, as Rosier tried to say that he'd tell his friend to speak with the dukes. He didn't flinch at the joke this time; he'd stopped grimacing as often in recent months. "Thank you. Run along now, duke."

"You could stay and help," muttered yet another duke.

"Don't listen to him," Baal replied to that and waved a hand at Rosier. "Go." Though Rosier wondered now what they'd been saying about him that Gemory misunderstood to mean that they needed him; maybe they'd been saying that they *didn't* need Rosier. 'I know that.' Nonetheless, he fought a frown as he turned and decided to return to his chambers. 'It really is Asmodeus who should've been a duke instead; he's far more helpful.'

On the way home, he passed by some demons carrying platters of food, all walking in a line — the scent of it hearty and strong and wonderful. It was enough for Rosier to breathe easier. He would eat well today, if nothing else. And so he lifted his chin as he reached the door to his room, tugging it aside, then slipping in. Yanking it back into place behind him, Rosier saw that Asmodeus was, as he'd said, in bed, laying flat on his back, his limbs comically spread like he were a dead animal, and Rosier couldn't help a chuckle. "Asmodeus."

A groan responded, but it sounded more moody than painful.

"Are you awake now? The dukes said they wanted to talk to you, something about construction."

With a swing of his legs, Asmodeus yanked his body up to sit, revealing a tired face and mussed hair. "Yes, but I've been trying to stop feeling tired. Should I get better dressed? Do I really have to go to this festival or whatever it is that Lucifer is up to? What if you and I stay in? We can play a game." They had a few puzzles on boards, some rocks, and targets — the kind of juvenile little things demons made to pass the time. "I won the last time we played anything. If you want, I'll beat you again."

Rosier made his way over with a blooming smile. "But you

said you wanted to go yesterday, and you won't feel any less tired if you're in the bed like that."

"Hm." Asmodeus rubbed at one of his eyes with a mangled, clawed hand. "Fine. Why not? Let me dress myself. How do you like me best? In the red or white robe?" He paused, the gaze of his obstructed vision on the fallen angel of fruit beside him, then he lowered his hand, reaching to take Rosier's wrist. "Or maybe I'll surprise you."

Rosier laughed a second time, then he turned his hand to grip at Asmodeus'. "How so? I live here."

"You're not going to return to the dukes?"

"I'm not sure." Rosier knew he wasn't needed, and yet he realized that he really could return to them, try to help. He just wasn't sure if he wanted to. "I think I'll only be in their way."

"Aren't they setting up for this festival? If you want to go help, you should. No need to be the demon of decor to put food on a table." He tugged on Rosier's hand, then pecked his lips. "Or stay here with me. Do whatever you like as long as you're happy."

Softly, Rosier smiled. "Thank you. I think I may try to help the dukes then." He tilted up his face and kissed the tip of his friend's nose. "You should stand up now so that you don't fall back asleep."

"I'm wide awake now," Asmodeus chuckled warmly, squeezing Rosier's hand before removing his touch and scooting away from him. He planted his feet on the ground, stood, wobbled — but his legs were firm today, and he limped toward a corner of the room without the help of his canes. "I'll meet you at the festival. Is that alright with you?"

"Yes," said Rosier, adjusting his tunic and breathing in slow, feeling much better than he had a mere few minutes ago. He headed back out, this time with a little bit of a hurry so that there was still something he could help with. As it turned out, there was. Stumbling into the hall, he saw that the platters of food were being reordered, that Baal was giving out contradictory commands, and that a duke had just shoved him back with a biting insult. Immediately, Rosier tried to get in between them, facing Baal, and suggested: "Let me help. I can rearrange the food and organize some things better. May I?"

Baal stared with wide, baffled eyes, but then gave his blessing.

As the day continued, Rosier had demons move tables, set the food platters in the most reasonable order, and he had the drinks placed in a separate area so that there wouldn't be too much traffic around the food. He, also, picked out a few decorative flowers on the cushions and tucked them into his hair. The dukes, who'd been simply following his lead, chuckled at this but didn't make any rude comment. 'I hope they think I look nice, despite their laughs.' Baal patted his shoulder, either in pity or comfort.

It wasn't very long afterward that said great duke handed out the order for the crowd of demons outside to be let in. Rosier took this to mean the celebration had begun, but he didn't really know what to do, where to stand, and above all else, he dedicated his time to scanning the area, searching for his closest friend. Above, the sunlight was dimming, and a duke ordered those closest to him to light the charcoal bowls placed on rocky, short columns.

At the same time, instruments of bone and string were beginning to sound and voices followed. The music was not how it had been in Heaven; it was still fast-paced, heavy in its beats, but the songs were now about pain and about pleasure, about fucking, and about gore. Swaying, Rosier focused on the rhythm alone, hardly noticing when the dukes around him began to scatter, to join friends to talk with or smoke, maybe some of those they'd led in wars during the earliest years on Earth. When Baal began to wander, Rosier followed like a shadow. Where was Asmodeus? Again, Rosier scanned across the hall, but his friend, who was rather tall and easily noticeable, was nowhere. Baal, meanwhile, joked with a demon about Satan having been an anxious, angry beast in the morning, though oddly distant as well.

Rosier raised his face at that. "What was he angry about?"

Baal shrugged. "I think he's afraid of this festival not working." As he said this, the curly-haired demon he'd been speaking to turned his attention to the chalice in his hands, drinking slow, moaning around the murky, fermented drink.

"Working?" Rosier realized how strange this festival truly was. "What is he... trying to do?"

"You noticed it, didn't you?" Baal crossed his arms, leaning down a little, the volume of his voice dropping to near whisper. "Some demons are getting too restless. They miss the wars from before Satan woke up. Moloch was encouraging them to act on all the shit they wanted to do. Lucifer told me that demons will start going against him if he doesn't do something."

Rosier breathed shakily, "But how will this fix things?"

There was a pause, only a few seconds long, with music and chatter filling the space in between, then Baal carefully answered: "You weren't there. You weren't there when Lucifer... corrupted us. He wants to recreate that or, I suppose, remind everyone." He shifted his weight, rolled his shoulders uncomfortably. "Remind us that we fell... not for war but for the pleasure that created it." Rosier blinked curiously; those were oddly sage words from Baal, whose cheeks had flushed a faint pink.

Before the fallen angel of fruit could reply, however, there was the clacking sound of a familiar wooden cane right nearby, then Asmodeus' voice saying, "Still hasn't started, I see." He nudged Rosier's arm and snickered. "I hope you didn't miss me for too long." He was dressed in a thin, dark-red tunic with some silver rings on his fingers, as well as beaded bracelets trailing up his forearms. "I forgot to give you something." With the claws that didn't grip his walking aid, he slipped a few fingers into the pocket of his robe, then tugged something out and pressed it to Rosier's lifting hand. Dangling in gold and blue — a necklace with filigree accents between sapphire gems. "I had to adjust the chain earlier, but I hope you like it."

Warmly, smiling, Rosier took and let it drape from his fingers. "It's beautiful. Thank you, Asmodeus."

Baal grumbled, "Where'd you get the sapphire?"

"I fucked someone for it," Asmodeus answered mundanely. "How else?" Rosier's lips twitched, but he didn't allow them to frown, especially when Asmodeus inched closer and spoke again. "Did I miss anything? I see Satan isn't here yet." He took the necklace again and, swift, draped it across Rosier's neck before clicking it into place at his nape.

"He should be here soon," Baal replied, then nodded his head. "Look, there he is." Instantly, he sighed, slow and adoringly, "Our beautiful, beautiful devil."

Lucifer, indeed, was crossing the hall, making his way past the middle of it with every demon scrambling out of his way, though many bowed their heads and some placed their hands together like they'd soon pray to him as they did to God in Heaven. Loudly, his jewels rattled as he moved, each chain hanging wantonly from him, his body covered in a sheer, ivy-green tunic that obscured not a hint of those legs, those hips, that waist, his chest, and the temptation of all temptations. Though some links of gold hung loose, there were some that instead hugged his figure, caressed it, pulled your attention to every little detail. On his head, Lucifer wore his crown of four horns, complimenting a cold, regal expression. Even for Rosier, it was unbearable to look at him. Once, Rosier remembered, Lucifer would have agreed.

It reminded Rosier of alcohol. The taste had been foul on the first sip, but once he'd learned to take the burn, it was difficult to stop drinking. Delirium could be addicting, could be like a dream. Even in paradise, one could find themselves craving and dreaming. Satan had taught them that — the same Satan who now climbed up the steps toward his ceremonial, flowered seat. Though Rosier couldn't hear them, he could very well imagine how the petals were lovingly praising the beautiful fallen angel, the first sinner, how they wished they had lips so they could kiss him too.

But Lucifer turned away from them, faced his children with some of his tunic trailing long enough to sweep the steps he'd just graced with his bare feet. "Demons," he called, his voice strong and booming as the final flutes and strings halted at his presence. "All you who have come, I thank you. Not all demons did. Some chose to sleep, some have chosen to leave the caves and wander. I expect that next year, every single demon will join us, but for this first festival, I don't mind that it's only the most loyal. You're all the most deserving of my care. I hope you've all eaten. I encourage you to eat much more."

Nervously, Rosier glanced at Asmodeus beside him, but his friend's gaze was on their king.

"Do all that you like tonight. Indulge in anything you like. Indulge in what is good for your flesh." His voice was dropping, curling like a snake, coaxing. "And don't forget why you fell." With this, some in the crowd whistled, clapping their hands, a few even cheering. "Musicians, return to your instruments, offer us something to dance to." But before the songs had even begun again, Satan added, "Baal, duke, come forth. Too, come Abaddon and come Belphegor, and Minos." All the named dukes immediately approached, Baal walking the fastest, leaving his friends behind without a single hesitating thought. He stepped before even Abaddon, who'd been standing so near to the steps where Lucifer had settled the throne. "Come to me, like I'm the Father, and you're my angels."

"Yes, Satan," Baal said, and some of the other dukes echoed, but shyer, more perplexed than the fallen angel of flight. He dropped to a knee before the devil in total submission, one hand planted on the ground to steady himself. Peering down at his most adoring duke, Satan remained unimpressed, slowly settling to sit, legs spreading, making room for a demon or two in between. "Allow me," Baal worded in a pathetic beg, "to please you."

"Worship," Satan demanded, and as the other dukes also approached, Lucifer cupped the chin of one, tugged him down to a kiss that began with a flick of his tongue against a parting mouth, then he took a fistful of another demon's hair with his free hand — Baal, who let out a needy grunt. A third demon moved to his knees, as well, taking hold of one of the devil's ankles, then dragging his teeth up the shin, to the knee, before gnawing incessantly on the warm thighs God had molded. "Pray to me." The music was beginning again, a slower song than before. "Make sin with me." The devil's own breath hitched as one of his demons kissed at his neck and palmed between his legs. "Mm," he hummed, then pulled Baal up into a sloppy kiss as every other duke laid a hand on him to drag along the plains of his body.

'No.' Rosier took half a step back right before hearing a high gasp beside him, and he turned to see the curly-haired demon that Baal had been speaking with, now with a stranger behind him, pressed close to his back and rolling his hips, biting down playfully on his earlobe. Rosier jerked his head another way but found only other bodies, demons of all kinds, curling around each other, locking their legs, their lips. Groans, then strained grunts of pleasure as claws gripped at clothes and pried them apart to reveal already flushing, sweating skin. The several hundred in the hall — some moving onto the hard ground, but many sinking onto the abundant cushions set all around them, a few others taking to the tables, either on their backs or on their bellies, each curving their spine to any intruding organ, whether firm or delicate. 'No, no, no.'

Beside him, Asmodeus breathed harshly.

Rosier's gaze flickered over; two demons were running their mouths along his friend, tongues tracing every exposed stitch, then trying to kiss at his chest, his belly, his groin, and his thighs. 'Don't touch him,' Rosier wanted to say, but a pleasured whimper nearby had his face warm terribly, unsure if in only embarrassment or in the discomfort building lower than his navel — hot and swirling. But he didn't like it, maybe the other demons did, but he didn't. Barely, Asmodeus muffled a moan as he visibly bit down on his lip, taking the locks of one demon to guide their teasing tongue, flickering at the bloody stitching at his hip, toward that part of him that preferred to be tasted.

Even still, Asmodeus managed to say through clenched teeth, "Rosier, are you going to stay?"

Rosier blinked. Standing amid the rising sea of an orgy, he realized that he didn't have to be here. He could leave. He didn't have to watch Lucifer pleasured by several demons, each eating away at him. He didn't have to be eaten here. And yet, Rosier nodded his head, and he breathed quietly, "I should. It's the festival." Though he knew he needed to sit before anyone attempted to pull him under to drown in their depravity. 'Would I fight it this time? Or would I lay there quietly, hoping they'd devour me to the point of death?' "I'll sit. I might go to bed early, but you can... do as you like."

Asmodeus stared, but he didn't say a word as a third demon took his arm — Gemory, still as painted and beautiful as he'd been earlier— and shoved him onto a collection of cushions. Together with the others, Gemory moved to smother Asmodeus with kissing and desperate rolls of his hips. The lust demon's clothing was grappled, then yanked over his head, and the fallen angel of fruit thought, 'I forgot to tell you— I do like you in that red tunic. You look very beautiful in it. Your face looks sharper and your eyes darker.'

For entire minutes, Rosier watched, however empty his face might have shined by the charcoal fires. Two demons tried to kiss one another with the tip of Asmodeus' hardened sin between them, while Gemory playfully swirled his tongue against Asmodeus' and rut his sin against his thigh — the demon of lust scratching his entrance with a talon dangerously in response. 'His grunts are nice.' Reaching, Rosier took an abandoned chalice of alcohol, perhaps Baal's, off a table and sipped, the taste murky and bitter and burning its way down to his stomach. Some demons were smoking as they fucked; Rosier was thankful for it. With a fog growing denser all about, he could reel in a huff of sheepish consciousness, and it was a little easier, though not much, to stare at everyone writhing as if in pain, though it was pleasure that did the seizing. 'Maybe I should feel proud.' He found himself settling onto the edge of a stone table, walking his sight over to the throne where Satan had his legs raised and praised each demon who adored him incessantly, smearing him as if with blessed ointment. 'All of the demons are captive to this urge in them like animals, even Satan — but not me.'

That vain thought, however, faded as quick as it'd come. Rosier had never been a proud angel, and he wouldn't be a proud fallen one either. For him, there was nothing powerful about being different. With shaking fingers, he took another swing of the alcohol, listening to the orgy around him sing. 'What good does it do to try and think myself better than them? In the end, which one of us is happy?' When a snicker sounded, Rosier turned back to face a demon winking at him, jerking his head, perhaps inviting him to come touch. A claw trickled along the fallen fruit angel's arm immediately after, then a tongue dragged against his cheek, and Rosier shivered away from the demon's teasing. He tried to stagger far from the table, and succeeded, but not without seeing the stranger who snapped, "Stupid angel. You think you're so much better than us. Hopefully someone rapes you while you're here."

The words beat a horror into Rosier's chest, piercing his stammering heart to gush and bleed, almost up into his mouth. With both hands, he clutched his alcohol, frowning intensely, the sounds around him so loud, so wet, so gross, that he felt like clawing out his own ears. 'That's enough; I've done enough,' he insisted to himself. 'I should go before I'm hurt.' His feet hurried beneath him, trying to carry him far from any groping touch. Only the presence of Asmodeus could lure Rosier to stay, but the various cries of the demons muffled every sound Asmodeus made. Rubbing, kissing him, almost entirely obscuring Rosier's friend from the very world. Blindly, the fallen angel set the chalice down at his side, a sharp *clink* following, perhaps the drink falling over to spill. But Rosier didn't look back. He headed for the door, his breaths coming quicker, airier.

There were other familiar faces in the flood of fucking, some demons he recognized as innocent, joyous friends in Heaven, now shouting out as they either rocked into another demon or were stabbed by sin, or both somehow. Rosier's stomach twisted in the sheer wrongness of it all, but even more disturbing was the crushing loneliness. He should be pleasing himself with the hands of a dozen demons. Or, at least, with Asmodeus.

Once he'd found his way outside, he rushed past the crowding in the halls as well, his vision blurred enough to make shadows out of the fallen creatures; Rosier told himself it was the alcohol, but it was not. Turning one way, he searched for any markers indicative of approaching his chambers, his face twisted angrily though he was already breathing easier just to be away from the chaos and lust. Without meaning to, he remembered the touch of his hands when he'd last watched Asmodeus partake in sin for an extended period of time, remembered how, for a brief moment, it had felt good. Fleeting, like the goodness had flown away from him before he could catch it. A tiny voice in his head said, 'Maybe you'll catch it next time, ride it to release like all the others. What's there, after the release? There must be some-thing if everyone's chasing after it and leaving me behind.'

Rosier found his door, slipped through it, and then pulled it closed. He kicked off his sandals next, trekked toward the center of the room, still panting, then flopped onto the bed in his flowers and jewels and tunic. Over his stomach, he laid a while, letting his eyes shut, trying to silence his thoughts so he could have a moment of his senses no longer so stimulated. In paradise, he had felt similarly with each festival. The fatigue, the ring in his ears, the spinning of the room. In that sense, Lucifer had really succeeded in bringing the demons back to Heaven.

Just some ten minutes later — "Rosier."

His eyes weren't closed, but they may as well have been with how he'd dug his face into the sheets. All Rosier could listen to was the clanking of a walking stick, the drag of the door, then a huff of exertion. Slow, he turned to rest his cheek on the mattress, staring with one eye at Asmodeus with his shivered hair, tunic torn at the front so that it'd been made like a robe. Some bracelets were missing, must've been stolen. "Asmodeus," Rosier whispered, rolling onto his back and staring at the ceiling, wanting to be sad or to be angry but instead feeling tired. "You shouldn't have followed me."

"You don't know... what they were saying they wanted to do to you."

"I do know." Rosier watched the skin of the mountain, like it might sag with age right before him or grow a lesion that'd dribble red droplets like wine into his open mouth. "I know." From his periphery, he could see Asmodeus with his head down, face hidden yet still reeking shame. "You should have stayed. You were having a good time, and you know that I don't... mind your habits. I think I'll sleep soon. I'll be here for when you come back." 'I'll always be here, Asmodeus.'

"For fuck's sake," Asmodeus grunted, and his knees bent a pinch, like he might double over, but his rage seemed directed at himself. "I don't know."

Tilting his face, Rosier stared at him firmly now, though his eyes were as distant as his voice when it whispered, "Do you want to fuck me, Asmodeus?" The demon of lust didn't move, didn't lift his face. 'I don't know why I'm asking. I know it. The first person you ever wanted to fuck was me. But I didn't let you.' "I'm sorry."

"Please. Don't apologize, Rosier."

Rosier was thinking again of the flicker of pleasure when he'd touched himself, and he was thinking of the trial with Moloch. "Can you... come closer please?" He, slow, lifted his body up to sit, just as his friend finally turned up his face, met his eyes with pain. "Come." He gestured, almost a little too mundanely. "I'm not angry at you."

"I wish you were," Asmodeus murmured, but he did as told,

walking with his cane, wavering a little but arriving eventually, standing right at the side of the mattress, just as Rosier scooted himself nearer, reaching to take Asmodeus' face in both hands. "Fuck, I wish you hated me. I wish you would have left me to suffer in some crater."

"I should be mad, shouldn't I?" Rosier conceded, but he leaned forward, pressing his lips to Asmodeus' gently. "Maybe I am. Maybe I do hate you a little." He reached to twiddle at a strand of long hair by one of Asmodeus' ears. "My heart hurts."

"I'm sorry."

"Kiss me," and Asmodeus did, quick, chaste. "Another time." Asmodeus pressed against him again, deeper. "I wish we could be better for each other. I wish kissing could fix whatever's wrong between us." Rosier sighed, knew that his breath was lapping at Asmodeus' mouth. "I don't know what to do."

"We can wash up," Asmodeus suggested. "Sleep." Like they always did.

'We all ought to be happy before the fires begin to burn,' Lucifer had said.

Rosier said, "I'm curious." He forced it out, then he forced out the next few words, "How it feels after it stops hurting." Strangely, it was terror that passed over the lustful demon's features. "If I'm allowed to close my eyes, I think... I want to try again." Close his eyes so that he didn't have to see Asmodeus' stare or God's. "I have nothing left to lose." He had nothing left to give.

"I don't want you to do it," Asmodeus said, "to make me happy."

"I want to do it to see if I can make myself happy." Rosier took one of Asmodeus' hands, placed it between his own legs how a demon had done to Lucifer, through his tunic, and exhaled again, quiet, more drawn-out. "I want to." He shut his eyes as Asmodeus nuzzled him, then leaned to graze his throat. "I want to." There was a curiously nice sensation trickling along his spine, squeezing his lower belly as if in a hug. 'Maybe only today, but I want to.'

"Let me eat you."

"Eat me?"

Asmodeus nodded against him. "It'll help." Rosier wanted to be helped, so he hummed affirmatively and allowed a peck against his lips. Immediately after, Asmodeus pressed the fallen angel of fruit against the headboard then climbed onto the bed with him, moving in between his legs. "And sucking always feels good too." He spit on his hand, then slipped it under the tunic to Rosier's arousal; instantly, the fallen angel gripped the sheets and twitched against the pillow cradling his back. The noise that fell out of his mouth was stifled, and he had to bite down another when Asmodeus' stroked his hand up, down again, then tugged Rosier's tunic upward to bring his face to that intimate place. His tongue draped out and ran itself up like a knife on Rosier. "But —" he said as Rosier arched his back and half-yelped at the sensation."Maybe I want you on top first. My lap." The lust demon's sigh was warm against Rosier's skin, only making him shiver some more. And Rosier felt an arm come around his waist and most of his back, tug him close as Asmodeus turned them around. Once again, they kissed.

Rosier angled his hips as he settled onto his friend's thighs, pressing his groin against Asmodeus'. The sensation was good, this much was good. Maybe he could lay here for some time, rubbing against Asmodeus, listening to his grunts, wait and see if the fabric of their clothes would dampen between them and ruin. He parted his lips, wanting to ask Asmodeus to be delicate because he didn't want this to hurt, but he feared the hurt was necessary. You can't fall from Heaven painlessly.

"I don't want to use my claws on you," Asmodeus said, cupping half his bottom with one hand, the talons nearly tearing the tunic, nearly sinking into soft flesh. "You'll have to finger yourself for me. I'll guide you." Again, again, Asmodeus kissed him; he pecked his cheeks, his jaw, then dragged his lips along his face. "Forgive me."

'I don't want to.' Rosier bit the inside of his cheeks and rocked against him, the stir of his building need making him flinch. 'But I'll still kiss you. Today.' Soon, he felt his friend taking his tunic and dragging it up Rosier's body slow, methodically, finally freeing him. 'Today, for if we burn tomorrow.' Nervously, he allowed Asmodeus to maneuver him upward enough that Rosier could easily set any part of himself over his friend's face or past the angel lips Asmodeus still carried with him.

The demon took his hand and guided it up to Rosier's mouth, slipping them inside. "Suck." Without arguing, Rosier wrapped his lips around his index and middle fingers, trying to disappear into the feeling of his friend's other hand tracing circles on his hip. The arousal between them was stiff, almost brittle. By the time Asmodeus tugged Rosier's hand back down, gripping the fallen fruit angel's wrist gently and making him prod the way in, his fingers dripped saliva like rain. "Work your fingers in for me."

'For you. Only you?'

Throughout the night, Asmodeus was careful, his hands coaxing, his tongue wetting. He spoke for the both of them, filling the gaps of silence between their dual breaths. Kissed him too much. And between the discomfort and the pleasure, Rosier found something that wasn't quite happiness; it was something new, something he wasn't sure of yet. He did cry, even choked up on it, but not out of sadness. He held Asmodeus tightly as he finished, a nice trembling trickling his thighs and hips for many minutes after the second-long death of release.

That morning, he woke with the taste of fruit on his lips.

CHAPTER 8

I n his hands, the fallen angel of fruit held a pomegranate. It had bloomed of a bright red flower from a cluster of them, almost like a shrub. It was born overripe — its scent too acrid, its inner coat too much the color of dried blood, its skin yellowing in parts, and its body bursting open, a few seeds having spilled to stain Rosier's fingers and pepper along the ground. In his mouth — there was the bitter taste of them. The first bloom of fruit. As it occurred in an unraveling miracle, there'd been a flicker of wonder that brightened Rosier's eyes, though now they remained in a daze.

Before him, the devil stared with parted lips, perplexed, furrowed brows, before he called, "Rosier," then took hurried steps toward him. "You've done it." His hand went to one of Rosier's, a cold touch coming over warm, stained skin. "A fruit. The first of many in our new paradise." A sweet, elated laugh sang from his smiling lips. "My dear friend, Rosier." Satan clamped both hands around the fruit now, leaning closer to the face of the fallen angel who was only half here, half understanding. "Our Earth will have beautiful fruit to eat. All the demons will sing your praises. You will bring us eternal harvest. "

"We can," whispered Rosier, "plant orchards everywhere."

And Satan's golden gaze flickered to the fallen angel of fruit's; their eyes were a similar sunny hue, but Rosier's eyes were more like dimmed sunset, perhaps darker than they'd been in paradise, while Lucifer's were the morning itself. "We can. We'll plant all the beautiful orchards everywhere that I promised you, Rosier." He leaned in quick, pressing his pursed mouth to Rosier's forehead. "I swore to you once that we would create our own paradise, and now we will have it."

Rosier hesitated, but then he felt a breath slip from his mouth how blood might from a wound. It took the form of an echo: "We will have it."

"Tell me," Satan pressed, "how did you do it?"

"How did I make the fruits grow?" Rosier asked softly, feeling Lucifer's touch stray from him. "I'm not sure. These last few days... my palms remembered the skin of fruit, the texture and its juice. I started dreaming of peaches and oranges, and I started tasting strawberries in my mouth every morning." Steady, the devil's gaze maintained itself on him, then climbed along his body, as if taking it in for the first time. When they'd met, Rosier had called the angel Satan beautiful, and the most beautiful angel had said Rosier was beautiful too. All the angels in Heaven were beautiful, though maybe some more than others. God had not made all angels equal; He could not make equals. He had, however, come very close, perhaps accidentally — had created some angels that saw so much of themselves in each other and created love in response.

The devil spoke again: "Have you been loving?"

"Loving?" Another echo.

"Have you been loving another demon?"

"I've always loved him."

"I see."

A frown turned the ends of Rosier's lips downward, and the pomegranate in his hands bled over his fingers. "Even before I met him, I think I loved him." His voice sounded far, as if up on a cloud, but Rosier knew where he was, could feel the moist, crumbling soil beneath his feet. 'I wonder if you could understand that. We angels don't know the future, but we can feel it, at times. I felt the love I'd one day have for my friends the day I was born. I can feel the grief of the coming years, too.'

"You will learn better," said Lucifer, but he took the pomegranate, then sunk in his nails to tear it apart and gather the seeds. Some messily spilled onto the ground between them. And, soon after, he said that the animals would come eat each seed, and they would carry them throughout the Earth. The fruits of Heaven had been cared for, but here on Earth, they would grow everywhere, and they would rule the world alongside them. Lucifer would offer to the flowers and fruits all the power that the Lord had denied them in Heaven. But Rosier knew that his pomegranate wanted no such thing; he knew the fruits.

Rosier found a little comfort in that. He may not crave power — how Lucifer seemed to think all living things did — but he was like his fruits — merely wanting to live and offer their bodies to break in someone's mouth. Rosier often did come apart in Asmodeus' mouth, now. "I think that I should go." He didn't know what else to say, even if he should be overjoyed to see that he'd created, birthed a pomegranate from his own touch, his body. 'The happiness will reach me another day.' For now, he was merely relieved. 'I'm still an angel of fruit. The angel of fruit. I was born with the taste of peaches in my mouth, and very soon, I will feel them on my tongue again.'

"Come back to me tomorrow, Rosier. There's still plenty to be done."

Rosier returned home then, to his room. There was a new tunic he was finishing the hem on, and once he'd made his way back, he wasted no time in moving toward his work by the hearth. As he fiddled with thread and needle, he also treated himself to a little liquor to feel his muscles lax beneath his skin and his worries fade into a fog of ease. When the door opened again, he hardly noticed, all his focus on his work and the crackling of the hearth. It was only once there were arms coming around him and the press of a body behind his, settling onto the same floor cushion, that Rosier lifted his head to meet the face of the demon he'd fallen for, but Asmodeus had just moved his mouth to his throat. It fluttered with a dead pulse.

"Ah," Rosier sighed, setting aside his tunic. He was already shifting to unfold his legs and spread them on the ground, parting them just an inch, as one of Asmodeus' hands wandered down his waist to his thighs, squeezing him there, so narrowly close to the place that Asmodeus liked so much, liked tasting and touching.

"How did," Asmodeus' purr rumbled against Rosier's neck, "today go?"

Rosier didn't want to talk, so he lifted some fingers and ran them through Asmodeus' hair, then scratching a little at his scalp gently until the older one grunted to stifle a relaxed moan. Asmodeus pulled away a second later, climbed onto his feet, then briefly touched the younger one's shoulder in a silent request to stand and join him in bed. They had fucked in the morning — Asmodeus loved it in the morning, and Rosier liked being drowsy enough not to mind — and they often did it two or three, even occasionally four, times a day. That was Asmodeus' appetite, at least, and Rosier was like his peaches, his pomegranates — just happy to be eaten.

This time, Rosier was bent over the mattress. And, soon after, he was feeling his friend's panting against his hair, murmurs in between of "Rosier, darling Rosier." Asmodeus rocked inside at a steady pace, and all the fruit demon could do beneath was clutch at the sheets of their bed. He never quite got used to the feeling of something inside, but when it pressed in deep enough, there was a whip of pleasure that shuddered his body and had a sound fall from his lips. There was a coiling need in his lower belly, the twitching and needy sin that he wanted to crush and spill from at once. When being half-asleep wasn't an option, drinking tended to help. Drunkenness made it much easier to enjoy the fullness and intimacy of being closer to his friend than he could have ever imagined, without thinking too long about his body or about how dirty this was.

Asmodeus always liked how dirty it was, how it stained them both.

Rosier bit down a noise as Asmodeus whispered praises in his ear, touching him, stroking him at the front, urging him to find release with him. It felt good. Truthfully, it nearly always felt good, and when it didn't, Rosier thrashed and Asmodeus would immediately stop. But, if this was true, and if it felt good so often, then why was Rosier frustrated? In theory, he could understand Asmodeus, could understand all the other demons now, and yet he didn't. 'I wouldn't kill for this, nor fall for it.' He leaned on his forearms and arched his back as Asmodeus' hips rocked in faster and took a hold of his upper waist. Listening to the beating together of their bodies, Rosier tried not to think of how desire was tearing him open at his pelvis. But, with a gentle hand going over his chest, Asmodeus tugged him upward so that Rosier's back pressed against his beastly front. "Hngh," he whined, and Asmodeus laughed warmly. In that position, with just a few ruts more, they finished.

Once, Asmodeus had asked if Rosier minded the semen inside him — mentioned there were some demons who hated it — but Rosier said it was his favorite part really. Not the clean-up, but the second of warmth and fulfillment and intimacy. If fucking was only that, then he might want it more often. But it wasn't. However tender Asmodeus' touch might be — delicate hands stabbing you are still ultimately stabbing you. You can kill someone just so gently before it's kinder to be rough and quick, to run a blade jaggedly across their throat than to bleed them out.

As usual, Asmodeus didn't hesitate to wash up with Rosier afterward. He cradled him for just a minute, then pulled him off the bed and tugged him to the corner of the room where they kept the water bucket and stone and soaps. Rosier allowed himself to be guided onto the stool, still feeling his chest rise and fall with tired breaths stuttering past his lips. Blinking, blinking, he couldn't do away with the mist over his eyes, and so he merely sat, obedient, and dipped his head forward to allow Asmodeus to wet his hair, then begin lathering at it, working each sud through the threads, careful with his tender scalp. "I," Rosier attempted, then found his throat so dry that he had to gulp and begin anew. "I grew a fruit today." Talons on his crown twitched, stopped moving. "It was a pomegranate." As his friend drew back his hands, Rosier saw a droplet dribble down the side of Asmodeus' face to dip beneath his jawline, roll down his neck and toward the line of stitches connecting him to a torso that was partly scaled and partly skin stripped of fur.

"How?" Asmodeus quirked a brow. "From nothing?"

"Not from nothing, from a flower." Rosier's gaze continued trailing down Asmodeus' body and saw, then, a hanging minuscule string sweeping down from his thigh — a stitch that had come loose — as well as blood turned pink dribble by their feet. "I don't know how I did it. I wouldn't say I meant to this time any more than the last attempts." He thought out loud: "I wonder if maybe God didn't mean to create. I never considered that. We always say that He created with so much intention and care, but maybe not... Maybe we're all an accident. Maybe He never wanted us at all." Asmodeus returned his hand to Rosier's head, but he scratched, he petted, he caressed and stroked, and the younger one's gaze flickered up to catch his friend's face. It was difficult to read, though tender in the eyes and lips pressed together, like he was preventing himself from saying anything so Rosier could keep chattering. "I'm happy." But Asmodeus' purring voice was always nice to listen to, and Rosier wanted to hear it. "Are *you* happy?"

The greater demon chuckled. "I'm amazed. You created like God, and you did it on purpose." His hand trailed to Rosier's mouth to trace its shape. "But I'm only happy if you are." When Rosier pursed his lips at him, Asmodeus grinned wider and added, "I'm simple. My darling friend is happy, and I'm happy."

"Would you feel the same way about Baal?"

"Baal's hardly a friend," Asmodeus laughed.

"He thinks otherwise, I'm sure."

"Demons can think what they like. There's only one darling friend that I have."

Rosier should've stopped his mouth: "The angel of friendship only has one friend?"

"The angel of friendship is dead," replied the demon, then kissed him. "Look at him rotting, Rosier." But the fallen angel of fruit realized his heart had slipped from its cradle, plunged into his belly like it were as damned as the body that carried it. "And he never was much of a friend to all the angels in Heaven, was he?" 'Maybe your purpose was never in Heaven but here, damned and waiting to burn. How can that be? How can you have found yourself only after dying?' "You're incredible. Can you show me the pomegranate? I want to see." His mouth worked quickly, pressing in deep like he wanted to climb inside and lay all of his weight over Rosier's tongue. "Mm."

Sighing, quiet, flinching, Rosier inched back and away. "I'm tired, Asmodeus." He shut his eyes for a moment to try and avoid how the demon might frown; he didn't want Asmodeus to think he'd made him uncomfortable, but Rosier was feeling his body slump. "Can we sleep?"

"Of course," Asmodeus said quickly, softer, taking his hand and squeezing it. "Of course," he echoed, "Rosier." He whispered his name like he wanted to keep it a secret between them, longingly like he didn't already have Rosier, under lock and key. Quickly, he cleaned the rest of him, soaping the younger one's limbs and carefully washing the place he'd spilled inside of.

Soon after, the fallen angel of fruit climbed to his feet. He went for the folded cloths they used to dry themselves with, expecting for Asmodeus to follow, but the older demon started hissing behind him, the kind he always did when he was clenching his teeth as tight as he could. Craning his face back, Rosier saw his friend shake his head, then rise to stand with insecure, wobbling knees, his hand going over his side. He gripped it, though there nothing visibly wrong. Yet. Rosier always did hate to see Asmodeus like this after they slept together; he often wondered why Asmodeus liked sex so much at all if pain often punished his sin.

"Go ahead to bed," the older one croaked. "It's late." What did that matter? They were in the caves, so far from sunlight. Even the stars couldn't see them. "I'll join you in a minute. I'm going to go out and find something for the pain. I'll be back." Rosier nodded, moving to begin drying and not saying another word. This was all becoming routine now.

Appropriately, the next morning began as it always did. The fallen angel of fruit woke to arms around him and a face pressing to, breathing hot against, his throat. Rosier touched Asmodeus' hair, waiting. When his friend began to stir, Rosier allowed his eyes to flutter shut once more, and he parted his dry lips already, patient for when the kisses would come. A clawed hand dragged against his side, climbing up, threatening to tear the tunic and plunge into Rosier's sternum and pierce his heart. Except, he was gentle — Asmodeus was — and slow; he hadn't hurt him yet. Rosier could even push his friend away, had every chance to say that he didn't want this — but Rosier always chose silence instead.

Once, Asmodeus directly asked, "Can I fuck you?"

"Don't ask," Rosier had murmured. "I don't want to answer. Just try it."

"I want to be sure."

"I'll never be."

So Asmodeus had learned not to ask, had learned Rosier wanted nothing less than a definite decision. His answer, after all, could change at any instant. Maybe he wanted it one second, then he didn't another. He always wanted the escape open, wanted the question to hang overhead like a guillotine, just in case.

As the two of them were in bed, Asmodeus kissed him softly, reaching down to run his hand along Rosier's front then work some circular strokes at the tip, and Rosier made soft noises for his friend, just enough to feel him go from already-firm to hard. Then, he tried pulling away to turn onto his belly. Rosier didn't like being on his back and facing God, and it reminded him, too, of that night the angel of friendship died right on top of him. He never told Asmodeus, though, that he preferred being on his hands and knees, even now as Asmodeus laid on him and took hold of his legs; he never told Asmodeus anything, really. 'I want you to be happy with me.' The lust demon held Rosier in place and was quick to begin trying to loosen and wet the way in, oil at its typical place on the ground by the bed, if needed. It was a new day.

Rosier was mostly quiet as Asmodeus relieved himself, though a few breathy groans of pleasure did escape. He allowed himself to be sleepy, nuzzling his friend and half-dreaming of making more fruits. He didn't finish, though he reassured Asmodeus that he didn't really want to this morning.

Some hours after they ate, they went to a lounge to spend some time, and Baal joined them. With a leg tucked underneath him, wearing a clean, thin tunic, Rosier sat on a straw-stuffed couch against the wall and played with the lit roll of herbs Asmodeus had just handed to him. In the corner of the room — fucking. As usual, as always. Two demons, neither of them recognizable, but Rosier watched them. 'I'm no different than you now, am I?' Asmodeus was in a tunic as well, taking a sip of water, and he was watching too. Gripping the top of a cane, his hand twitched.

Baal was snickering at Asmodeus' other side and picking his teeth with an animal bone before a demon sitting on the chair of the couch tugged at his arm and purred into his ear. And before them, one of the two in the midst of fucking turned over and called out: "Asmodeus, come join! Show us your cock!" Then, lower, more accusing, he added, "You... never come to the orgies anymore."

Rosier stared at the blunt in his hand, wishing now there was something stronger, something that could numb him a little more.

"I can't," Asmodeus said.

"Who has you punished?" the oblivious Baal laughed over at him just as he was moving down to his knees so he could suck at the towering, gorgeous demon with twisted horns who was pestering him.

Bringing the herbs to his mouth, Rosier breathed in all his troubles and expelled them through his nose, feeling Asmodeus' gaze on him and realizing they'd been too hasty to clean earlier. He was wet still, inside, some dead seed lingering. "Come, Rosier," said the one who'd fucked him. "I wanted to see the... creation you told me about." He squeezed his shoulder, and a demon nearby scowled. "The weather outside is nice today, I hear." Asmodeus took the blunt from Rosier's mouth, stubbing it on the couch and flicking it at the orgy who'd still been staring longingly at him. "We can drink and smoke later."

Rosier nodded, then squeezed his friend's hand as it took his own. The cries and growls in the room continued as they rose to stand and headed for the exit. Breathing a little sigh in relief, Rosier listened to the noises fade the second they traveled out, each step they took muffling the sound of the lounge further. "Thank you," he thought to whisper, even happier to see that the corridors were quiet today.

"No need to thank me." Asmodeus leaned down and kissed his hair. "Will you take me to the pomegranate that you were telling me of? I understand if you don't want to."

Rosier smiled gently at that. "I would really love to." And after they walked out into the breezy, half-clouded late summer day, he tugged Asmodeus along, trying to bring him to the meadow where Lucifer always waited for him. He even let go of Asmodeus so that he could hurry ahead and ensure the devil wasn't there to disturb them. What Rosier met, instead, was many flowers, open and welcoming — but not a fruit in sight. "Oh," he said, "Lucifer must have hidden it away."

"Hmm," was the response from the demon approaching behind, "then maybe we should look for him."

"Well," said Rosier, crouching to touch one of the flowers, the petals smooth and kind. "Wait a moment." He stroked it, rubbed a finger against the perfect yellow sun in the middle, smearing nectar, and when he turned his hand, a fruit fell against it. This time, it was a peach, bright and orange as sunset, its skin as soft as the hand that held it. "Ah," he said much more excitingly than when he'd been with Lucifer. "I did it again. A fruit." Just as he lifted his face, Asmodeus was nearing him, limping along with his cane's support, his eyes nonetheless wondrously wide at something that was like the heart of Heaven, created now on Earth by his fallen angel friend. "You see? I've done it..."

"You can create," Asmodeus said, "like God."

"No, and I feel like..." Rosier spoke his thoughts aloud, as he'd done to him the night before, "it's temporary. I feel like I'll return to bearing no fruit soon, like there's only a few in me. I'm... recreating how I recreated you. From parts, from what God has left here. Once I've made a few of them, I'll never be able to make more." He lifted the peach to his mouth, and he pressed his teeth onto its skin, feeling how it came apart slow before he bit a piece off cleanly. Chewing, he knew that this was not the taste of Heaven, but something close. Lucifer had said they'd create a better paradise outside of Heaven, and though that wasn't true — it did seem they could get very close. After he swallowed, Rosier outstretched his hand, and he watched Asmodeus lean down, put his mouth against where Rosier's had been, his tongue running over the indents, the juice spilling onto his lips, dribbling down his chin, trailing like tears down his neck.

"Mm," Asmodeus bit down, taking a larger piece than the one the younger of the two had taken. "It's good. Really good." His sigh was happy though harsh, and then he laughed. "I didn't realize how much I missed fruits."

Rosier smiled again; his eyes squinted happily. "I want to cut a fruit for you. The next one, I'll cut for you."

"Let me do it," Asmodeus insisted, swiping now the peach from Rosier, bringing it up to his mouth and messily gnawing at the rest of it, using his claws to stab into the dark pit, then drop it to the floor. "Fuck, it's so good." Rosier's laughter was bright before he tried to reach for Asmodeus' hand again, to examine and check if there were any peach pieces caught on the stitch-work, only for Asmodeus to lean down, swiftly, and kiss Rosier deep on the mouth. The taste in between them was so sweet that they really could have been angels again.

And though Rosier was happy, he found his smile faltering when he realized Asmodeus was pulling him to the ground. Sex, again. The flowers made a soft bed beneath them, their bodies tickling the sides of his face, his neck, his feet. But Rosier breathed in, grabbed at Asmodeus' arms and reciprocated the kissing, trying to ignore the churning nerves in his stomach. He would try to finish this time, with him. He didn't want to ruin such a nice moment. "I love you, Asmodeus."

"I could eat you alive, Rosier," was the warm chuckle in response.

Rosier supposed now was the time — he tasted like a wonderful peach — so he held Asmodeus tighter and waited to see if he would. But he did not.

An hour later — they both found release. And, as he did, Rosier began to wonder if he'd one day forget what it felt like to be empty inside. If he would forget what it was like not to drip and have to be cleaned, to only know to drip again, again. It made him think of the peach with juice spilling down Asmodeus' mouth. He thought of himself, dripping from Asmodeus' mouth. He flinched, though he felt good. It usually felt good. How to explain that to Asmodeus? It was good, but not good enough for his full attention, not good enough to always enjoy. How to explain it to anyone?

Rosier began to smoke more. It helped. Asmodeus doing it with him helped, too. And the more he fucked Asmodeus, the more he drank.

THE SEVENTH MEMORY

In Heaven, before Asmodeus, Rosier had seldom suffered loneliness. He had friends, though none of them particularly close, and he met many angels, who often noticed him in the orchards and shared chuckles. They laughed because he liked to sleep tangled between the dark roots. "You should find a house to sleep in," someone urged him, but Rosier said he liked to rest with his body against the bark of an apple tree, gazing up at the red fruits and counting every dimple on their skin. Even still, countless offers continued to come — strangers inviting the fruit angel to their spare beds or even promising to help build an entire home if he wanted to be alone. After a hundred thousand years, the angel Rosier tired of making excuses, and his friend Azazel was especially stubborn, so he surrendered and went on to move into Azazel's crowded home for a few years.

One of the workspaces on the second floor would be converted into a bedroom for him, Azazel reassured, then continued to reassure as Rosier had to share his bed for the time being. Smiling, Rosier always said he didn't mind. It was true — the bed-sharing wasn't much of a problem, though Azazel's home didn't seem right for him. Shouting and laughter made the walls constantly shake, and Azazel, for as much as Rosier liked him, was always talking, rather unaware of the times Rosier was desperate for silence. He snuck away when he could, returning to his trees, which spoke to him quiet enough not to overwhelm him. The angels who saw Rosier called him the angel of fruit. It may have been a tease, but there are many angels who find their purpose through the amusement of others, while some find themselves through awe. Rosier never believed he could awe anyone, but he had no desire to.

He dreamt little at times, didn't have anything to dream of. He was one of those angels who had everything he could ever want. The Lord was kind to him. The Lord was good.

One day, Azazel and Rosier were in the bathhouse, both of them sitting at the edge, mostly done washing and now simply lounging naked. Their bodies dribbled droplets, rolling down the plains and softer parts of their figures, glistening from the eternal shine that rained down from the atrium. To see each other nude meant nothing, nor did how handsome they found the details of their hips and legs and stomachs. Innocence had tasted like a smile around a berry. In between them, there was a small porcelain plate of such a thing — many berries, in fact.

Fingering two into Rosier's mouth, the angel who was without his face paint for once said, "I wanted to tell you something, brother."

"Mm?" Rosier crunched the berry between his teeth and watched two angels wrestling in the pool, one grappling the other around the throat and then pulling him down. Their great wings fluttered to toss water at those near to them, who groaned, but there were a few onlookers cheering them on. Angels had such lovely voices, perfect in pitch, throat-y and elegant.

"I know you don't like living with me." Before Rosier could speak through the rapid-forming frown over his lips — Azazel waved a hand and clarified, "I know you like *me*. I know we're friends. We are, aren't we?"

"Yes," answered Rosier, quick. "I think you're my best friend."

Azazel laughed at that, then nudged him playfully and leaned over to peck one of Rosier's warmed cheeks. "I'm very honored, but even if I'm your closest friend, I can very well see that you don't enjoy the house. And, to be honest, Samyaza has given me a hard time about that room I wanted to give you."

"He's very been strange with you lately."

"Hasn't he? Ah, well." Azazel shrugged and leaned back on his elbows over the tile, staring at the brawling angels with him. "But what can I do? Samyaza can be angry at me all he likes. It's none of my concern." Rosier nodded. "None at all." Rosier nodded some more, though slower. "But..."

"But?"

"Oh, nothing. Nothing, nothing!" Azazel huffed, then flopped to lay on his back and stare at the ceiling.

Rosier decided not to ask, and as he looked at the other end of the bathhouse, he noticed a figure far away from them, who was too tall with long dark hair. He thought nothing of him, and soon Rosier leaned to lay with his friend for some moments. Azazel was no fan of silence, but he didn't fill it as he usually did, and Rosier began to fear that maybe he was upset about something. "Forgive me, Azazel—"

"There's nothing to forgive you for, brother. You can live with me as long as you like, and when you leave, I'll be happy you've found the right home to hold you. I just want you to be comfortable."

"I'm not sure if I'll ever leave the orchards," Rosier mused.

"I'd be sad if you choose to sleep there forever, but I can't stop you. You're the angel of fruit, maybe that's where you belong." Rosier listened to angel chatter, angel joy. "I know that when God made you, you spilled out of a nebula like it was a fruit and you were a seed."

"Who told you that?" Rosier wondered, turning his head, the cold mosaic pressing against his cheek. "Raphael?"

"You told me," Azazel replied, then looked back at him with a kind smile, "though you might've been asleep."

"I didn't think I dreamt."

"We all do, sweet brother. You just don't realize it. You forget."

CHAPTER 9

Some years passed, and one day, it was winter. And Rosier was sitting on a wooden chair before a vanity mirror that Asmodeus had added recently to their chambers. He had no memory of how he got there, but he found himself staring at mussed hair, a pale tunic with a widened collar nearly slipping past a shoulder, a peppering of red mouth-shaped marks on his neck, and a pair wide, bloodshot eyes. They must've been teary, recently; though there were no ghost trails of tears along his face, his throat was horribly sore, feeling like it'd been scrubbed raw. His mind was hazy, his breath was herbal, his stomach burned. 'Where am I?' He blinked, then looked down, realizing his tunic was torn along the bottom, and the feeling of Asmodeus' soft kiss still tingled on a cheek. The echo of their last conversation was dancing about his skull:

"Rosier, I'll be back. The other dukes ordered me to help them with something — but I can bring you with me."

"No... No..." Rosier's voice drunken, high, and so wonderfully euphoric. "I want to sleep."

"Let me clean you, darling."

"Asmodeus... I love you."

And earlier than that, Rosier had been on his back, feet by his head, feeling himself come in and out of darkness, mind whirling with crystalline powder inhaled beforehand. He'd blink and find that entire minutes had passed unaccounted for. His moans would be nothing like the gasps that were spilling from his lips seconds ago. Asmodeus' mouth would be on him, then not. He would be smiling, then not.

Remembering it all now, the worst of it came back vividly — the feeling of hardness driving in, nearly out, then back in, the hold around it not as tense as it had once been. Asmodeus fucked him so easily now, had loosened him, shaped him the way Rosier had shaped Asmodeus' body as well. Immediately, Rosier lurched forward, stomach ripping to pieces inside, to vomit out a cry or perhaps whatever he'd drank and snorted and smoked to get as elated as he had. 'Rosier, Rosier,' God's voice had rattled in Rosier's head as he hugged Asmodeus during their second fuck of the day. 'Angel of fruit.' Fallen angel who'd brought his fruits down with him. 'You disgust me.' It was utter revulsion that made Rosier shiver, put a hand over his mouth, horribly conscious of the dried sweat on his skin, of the *stench* of sex — acrid and sharp as rot hanging off a branch. Fiery coughs ripped up his throat to the space behind his eyes, and he choked on the heat of his hysteric laughter, or was it cries?

'Oh, Father,' he wanted to mock at the mirror. 'You finally talk to me now? Now that I've stopped listening?' Though it must've been his mere imagination, been the high. Maybe if Rosier got high enough, he'd find himself in Heaven again.

'I never did care to meet you.'

'You only seek God when you want, and I never wanted. Not much. I never wanted much.' Gasping, he balled hands in his hair, yanking like he'd rip off what remained, tears scorching their way out of the folds of his eyes. 'I never wanted this.' He never wanted to feel these things, he didn't *like* these things— 'No, no.' He had to. He had to like it. 'God, what is *wrong* with me?' His head dipped forward as his terror continued to fall in unbridled downpour. 'Oh, what's wrong with me? Was I made too good for the demons? Was I too good for Heaven too? Don't I belong somewhere? Father? Father, I'm listening now. Please talk to me now.' He brought his hands to his face, and his fingers were trembling in smeared vision. 'Please, hold me. I'll do anything to return to you. I want. Finally, I *want*.' Finally, he was ready to meet God.

But there was no God on Earth, and so Rosier wept until his fingers pruned beneath his tears.

Until Satan, who was in his chambers with a small fossil — appearing like a split stone with the imprint of an intestine embedded circularly — heard the door behind him. He was crouched before the bonfire he kept against a wall — not a hearth, not quite — with a hollow gaze on the insect in his hands, dead for a hundred million years. He didn't move at the sound of someone entering the room, nor did he react to the quiet breaths of the fallen angel — perfectly, politely hushed. Familiar. "Rosier." He turned the fossil in his hands. "You've come at the right hour. I just sent some guards to escort Baal away from me." Nails digging at the groves, feeling the details of what had once been a body; was angel Lucifer fossilized within Satan as well? Was sweet, shameful Lucifer within the stone of a demon, waiting to be cracked open, to be found again? "Sometimes, I punish Baal just to see if he will accept the punishment. He always does." Lucifer turned back.

Tangled hair clouded the fallen angel of fruit's face, and he wore a long white tunic that swept along his ankles, sleeves over the arms hanging limply at his sides. Though he was slumped over, Rosier's reddened, wide eyes were on Satan, distant in their seeing. The shadows cast out from the fire whipped at his body like a breeze might, and as did the light. His honey irises shone, glimmered, like gold peeking from gray ore. "Lucifer," left his mouth, weak and broken.

Satan sighed, but then his eyebrows curved in pity or a parody of it, and he rose to stand, dropping the fossil he'd been examining haphazardly by the fire. "Come," he urged, lifting both spread arms in offering. "Rosier." He didn't approach as the smaller one idled, his face flickering frightfully. "You poor thing." But soon Rosier began staggering, almost hurrying, over to the devil's warm embrace, the neck that the fallen angel couldn't resist pressing his face to, breathing in the alluring scent of. However tinged it was with the metallurgic touch of blood, there was still lavender there, lilies — florals of the most pleasant kind.

A hiccup erupted from Rosier's mouth as he clutched at Lucifer's robe, his heart wringing itself out toward his tongue as the other stroked a comforting hand along his back. "I'm sorry." God wouldn't hold him, so he'd wandered to Satan instead. "I don't know why I came to you. I wanted to go to someone. I feel disgusting, Lucifer. I feel like there is mud all over me and everything is nauseating. I want to— I don't know what I want. I feel that I'm broken somehow, but I don't know anything else. I want to lay down. I want to rest." He shook his head before Lucifer had even asked. "But not in my own bed. I can't stand to be in my room right now." The fire crackled, clicked, filling the quiet between Rosier's uneven breaths.

Lucifer's fingers rose to choppy hair, and he scratched his nails slow, soothingly. "Come. Let me wash you."

"I've already washed," the fallen angel of fruit said. "No matter how many times I've washed, I feel dirty." He shut his eyes, and he felt his friend's touch begin to lull his heart and mind. "I'm sorry. I'm sorry again for coming to you."

"I told you that you came at a good hour, and I meant that." Turning his head, Lucifer pecked Rosier's temple. "If you don't want me to wash you, would you like a meal? I'll order a demon to bring us some meats, and I have an orange."

One of Rosier's fruits. "Yes. Yes, please." Rosier lifted his face, staring up at beautiful Lucifer, the nearby flames casting a glow around his head that made him an angel once more. "I hope you don't mind."

"I could never mind a friend." He tapped another kiss to Rosier's head. "Have some water and sit by the fire. I'll be back. If you want to change into something clean, you can wear a tunic of mine, as well." With the fingers that were still in Rosier's hair, Lucifer combed the knots. "I'll take care of this too." Delicately, he stepped away, and Rosier breathed a little easier as he touched his drapery and watched the devil turn on his heel, heading for an archway. As of now, Satan's chambers were quite simple, composed of only two spaces: a living area and a bedroom, separated by the mere stone arch. "Come. Follow me."

Rosier could see directly into the place for sleeping — the undone bed and the open cabinets and the spilling wardrobe. The clutter lured him closer, feeling his bare feet knock aside the fossil before he glanced down at it. "I'm," he began an apology again, so quiet that it faded into its whisper and never finished, before he returned his attention to the bedroom. A little part of him remembered young Lucifer and his messy room of a million gifts and a constant puddle of his tears. He imagined scolding the devil — the great Beast before him now currently pulling some clothing out to lay on the mattress — to clean, but he didn't dare. They were neither of those angels anymore.

At Satan's word, Rosier undressed, then pulled on some of Lucifer's furs and a tunic — a thicker one that was a bit long on him, that he had to tie at the back.

As this took place, the devil, indeed, ordered food for them, and it arrived within only a few minutes. After this, Lucifer and him spoke little, basking in silence on the ground before the fire. It reminded Rosier of the flames Asmodeus had lit when he'd run into the forest the day he'd tried touching himself, only to come away disgusted and miserable. It was odd to think of that day now — how he had promised not to have issue with Asmodeus sleeping with others, only then to decide he wanted Asmodeus for himself. Slowly, Rosier looked over, his eyes tired, to Satan who was fingering the small cuts of roasted meat on a plate between them, picking a few, then bringing them to his mouth. "Mm," he said.

There was a time that Lucifer had been dead on Earth, and

Rosier had taken care of him. During those years, Rosier would still call up to God, listening to the echo of his own voice from the sky. He'd prayed for wickedness not to be victorious on the land or on his soul, but he'd stopped praying one day, without even realizing it. And he had accepted evil into his life and past the shape of his lips without realizing it. It was easy to envy someone like Satan, who had fallen with vigor and intention; Rosier felt that demonhood had crept upon him, instead, like an opportunistic predator.

Tiredly, Rosier rubbed at an eye, then tugged on the fur draped over his shoulders. He shook his head when Lucifer outstretched a chalice of wine to him. "No," he whispered, "thank you." Though he expected Satan to argue, he instead pulled his hand back, shifting in his seat, and lifted the drink to his own mouth to sip. "I'm sorry," Rosier said anyway. "I drank too much this morning."

"You should eat more." Elegantly, Lucifer lowered the chalice, setting it by the platter, then took a piece of the seasoned meat. He brought it to Rosier's face, and though the fallen angel of fruit initially frowned, he soon parted his lips, allowed the devil's fingers to press the food inside. He hadn't been hungry, yet the taste rustled awake his belly as he chewed slow. A quiet, pleased noise — then he swallowed and shut his eyes for a moment. The fire continued crackling; the air chilled the back of his neck. "Don't starve yourself. There's no need." Another piece of meat soon pressed against Rosier's mouth, and he ate that too. "Good. Fill your stomach."

"We don't have to eat animals anymore," Rosier mused softly. "Now that there are fruits, we could return to how we ate in Heaven."

"But why eat like angels?" Satan asked levelly, and Rosier had no answer. "We're not angels anymore, though you and I might still seem to be. More you than me. Anyone will notice that there's something... frightening about my face, my body, something terribly wrong. But you're still missing your horns, Rosier.

Why?" Again, the fallen angel of fruit had no answer. "It's a shame. Some curved horns would complement you well. The devotion you have to the body God gave you is sad to see. I can tell that you don't like it — your body. No angel really does, and when they fall, they see the truth. They see their nakedness for what it is." Hesitantly, Rosier opened his eyes again, gazing into the fire. "Keep eating."

'Aren't you disgusted,' Rosier wanted to ask, 'to mutilate yourself?'

Lucifer's voice in his head replied, 'Don't I have the right? Don't we all have the right to mutilate our bodies? It belongs to me, not to God. I'll happily cut it to pieces if that means it won't look like the one my Father made for me.'

Once they'd finished, they went about blowing some candles to a dark, smoking death, but left the fireplace lit, and headed toward the devil's room to his rather enormous bed. Rosier shrugged off and set aside the furs he'd borrowed before crawling under the many layers of blankets, shuddering at the terrible chill surrounding them. Nearby, Lucifer was removing his robes to remain in a simple tunic, as well, before climbing onto the mattress with him. Rosier laid on his back, staring at the ceiling, his heart unsettled to feel himself in a different bed than the one he'd grown accustomed to since they'd moved into the caves centuries ago. When Satan approached, however, he shifted closer. Rosier's arms went around him, and their legs tangled; pressed together, their bodies built some cozy warmth.

"Mm." Immediately, Rosier was drowsy — the memory of his violent crying in the afternoon feeling far as horizon, the dinner curing a pain he'd neglected, and the devil's touch as wonderful as an angel's.

"Will you sleep now?" muffled against Rosier's hair.

"In a moment. I wanted to thank you. I felt so alone."

"Poor thing. You're such... a poor thing."

"And thank you for not asking what was wrong."

"I can sense when a demon doesn't want to say it."

"But I really do think there's something wrong with me. I think—" Rosier sighed weakly. "For years, I've been trying to enjoy pleasure. My soul won't allow it. It doesn't like it." He could admit to himself that *his body* liked it, at least most of the time — but Rosier must be separate from his flesh if his thighs could tremble in wonderful finish while his heart wept. "You're right that the fall has made me see my body and dislike it. I used to never mind any part of me, and now it feels like a rag that I carry. I wish that I were like you or Asmodeus or even Baal. I wish I could love the way pleasure makes me feel. I suppose true pleasure for me lies elsewhere, but I haven't found where it could be." He lifted his face and met Satan's stone, yet listening, gaze. "All I find is anger that I don't know what to do with. How terribly I want to direct it at you for creating this place and leading everyone on the path toward sin, but I can't bring myself to hate you. I held you in my house, I cleaned you and braided your hair. I can't hate that little angel, and so I can never hate you. But, please— Why did you do it, Lucifer? All of this? I've never understood."

"Why did I create sin?" Satan prompted, and Rosier supposed that was what he'd asked. "Hm. Who is to say? Of every angel and demon in Heaven and Earth, it's maybe only you who saw God hurt me." Instantly, all the muscles in the fallen angel tensed. "But who is to say what happened?" Some time before the war in Heaven, the most beautiful angel returned from God staggering, hurried to his bedroom, then he had sobbed inside in such agony, such distress and fear, that Heaven had never recovered from whatever wound was inflicted that day. "I am just a vessel for sin; what does it matter how it seeded itself in me?"

'Some other time, I wondered if Michael was the one who hurt you, who might've taken your legs and forced you apart and that is how you learned of love and sin at once, devil,' Rosier thought and so desperately wanted to say. 'But it was that day, after you returned from God, that you were never the same as before. I saw Him hurt you once; I should've known that He could have hurt you again.' But could God commit such an act? He couldn't; God has no interest in flesh. 'I shouldn't think of this ever again.' What a silly thing, to imagine God a rapist. 'He has no interest. I am being over-dramatic.'

And yet he couldn't help but think of God's hands on his own body, digging in until they sunk through the tendons and the muscles. He couldn't help but think of how their bodies had belonged to Him. How He had molded each one in splendor or boredom or loneliness. Angels were made for God's pleasure, if not in one way, then in another. He is fucking them all, whether they are on a bed before Him or hiding faraway among the stars. He's inside us all.

Lucifer reached out, swiping away some stray hairs over Rosier's cheek, then tracing the tear lines that had been there earlier. "One shouldn't think of the past or whoever you thought you first loved. Don't let yourself live a million years, then spend the rest looking back. Rosier, there is too much love in you. As long as you continue to carry it, you'll remain a dead angel on Earth."

"I've tried, Lucifer," Rosier confessed. "I've tried to be like all of you. I've fallen, but I can't do away with my love. It won't leave me even if it's hurting me."

"I know," Lucifer whispered, and he leaned their faces close enough that their breaths touched. "I know." The mirage of gold over his eyes reflected Rosier's own stare, and it did so for many faraway crackles of the fireplace. When his gaze flickered to Rosier's parted mouth, Satan said nothing, and he didn't speak as he brought his lips closer. The kiss was soft, initially, like the caress of a petal, then it split apart, pressed deeper. As it did, the fallen angel of fruit's eyes remained open, too wide. He watched as the devil kissed him delicately, like he would soon begin to show cracks under the weight. "Mm," Lucifer hummed against Rosier's mouth, whose lips pressed back only a little, only in confusion, for some short seconds. Then, Rosier drew back, slow, face blooming with bewilderment even when Satan's remained rather devoid of anything.

"No," left Rosier's mouth, hushed, then he shook his head, shame rising up his body like fever. "I'm sorry, Lucifer."

"You didn't like it."

"I'm sorry." Of course Rosier had liked it — how couldn't he enjoy the most perfectly shaped lips in Heaven and Earth? "But I don't want to kiss you like that. Forgive me."

"I don't understand," said Lucifer, firmer, "why you won't leave him behind. You don't like the way he loves you. He is no good for you, and he doesn't respect me."

Rosier swallowed, thick enough to suffocate. "I can't explain it."

"Why have you forgiven him for all that he's hurt you?"

"I haven't," Rosier admitted. "I just... would rather not think of it. I just want to be happy with him. We've been friends since before you were born, Lucifer. And I don't know if I can make you understand. I want to... love him, and I know that he loves me." The words softened his heart. "And I want us to find... a way to love each other right." He paused, scratching at the bedsheet with a little anxiety, before murmuring, "I know you don't love me like that either." Lucifer stared. "I hope you come to see that you don't have to sin with everyone you know. There are other ways to love, too, Lucifer." The devil shifted, turning onto his back. "I hope you can believe me."

"You will learn," said Satan, then murmured it a final time as his eyes fell shut. "You will learn through heartbreak."

When morning came, he was gone.

Rosier saw this, then laid in the devil's bed alone for an hour more, still wrapped up in all the blankets. Though Satan had seemingly not liked the direction the evening conversation had turned, the fallen angel of fruit had woken much calmer. He rose to sit, and he put his hands together, thinking of what he must do with new resolve. Climbing off the mattress, he went for his tear-stained clothing, removing the tunic he'd borrowed from Satan and setting it at the corner of the bed he decided to tidy for him, as well. He combed his hands through his hair, afterward, as he headed for the door, only to stop when he caught himself in a tall mirror by the wardrobe. He made note of his body shape, the uneven cut of his hair, his face, his limbs — all these parts that his lover seemed to adore so much, that he couldn't see what was so alluring about. He half-turned, curious of what Asmodeus saw when he had him bent over, only to sigh. 'What have you ever seen in me, Asmodeus? What do you like about this body? What do you like at all about bodies?' The next thought came as a realization: 'It's the first morning in so many that I'm not having sex with him.'

It was nice. He felt happier, lighter.

Rosier crossed his arms and rubbed at them to try and fight the cave coolness as he stepped out of the devil's chambers. He felt that, all things considered, he didn't mind being liked. He supposed he didn't mind that Asmodeus loved his body, either. Being loved by Asmodeus was something he wanted, he was sure of that. There was no one else that he wanted love from, not even from the most beautiful creature of all. But Rosier couldn't fill Asmodeus' appetite, either, so what was there to do?

Out in the corridors, cheers and claps were drowning all other sounds, and very soon, Rosier saw that the noise was following the short-haired beast of Moloch, still in his prisoner rags but without a cuff or collar. In the center of a crowd, Moloch outstretched his arms and swiveled his body, pointed teeth all shining in a monstrous grin. Rosier, watching demons shove playfully at Moloch, only then remembered that he'd been due to leave the dungeon this year, and he must've been set free today. Right nearby, grumbling sounded, and Rosier turned to see a demon wrapped up in a shawl — a tall blonde with a scowl on their face and furious twitching eyebrows — Gemory. Rosier immediately frowned and tried touching his wrist. "Are you well?"

Sharply, Gemory replied, "Get away from me!" and shoved

Rosier's arm hard enough to make him stagger in place. "Don't you dare speak a word, duke. What do you want to say? Do you want to say you're sorry?" A bark of a laugh. "I don't want your comfort. I want that war-loving shit eater to suffer." Rosier frowned, but he didn't know what else to say as he cradled the hand that'd been pushed aside. "Well," Gemory huffed, "I suppose that's the bad part about living with demons. They're all horrible fucks. Satan only punishes them when they take it too far, but everyone here is a horrible fuck." A forced, almost frenzied grin rose to his mouth, and through a laugh, he repeated, "I don't want your comfort. You can stand there, and you can *pretend* to be bothered. But if you really cared, you would do something. But you never do." He began turning on his heel.

"Gemory—"

"Be *quiet,*" was the hiss in response as Gemory twisted his head back at the fallen angel. "How annoying can you be? Stop making that stupid face, stop talking in that stupid voice. Stop trying to act like you're any better than the rest of us when you sit with your legs crossed in the corner of the room. You're not any different from us — do you know that? You think you're still an angel, but you're a sad little demon in denial." Rosier startled but parted his lips again to speak. "Get the fuck away from me, duke. Act helpless and cry and do nothing, just know that a demon who doesn't kill or fuck is still a demon. There are *no wings* on your back." Instantly, Rosier's body cooled inside even colder than he felt on the outside; the open gashes on his back stung. "And you're going to burn like the rest of us whether you beg God to spare you or not." With a shaky inhale, Gemory finally shut his mouth, stumbling back, and then hurried to walk in the opposite direction of the commotion and Rosier.

"Moloch!" someone was yelling. "Do you think Satan will restore you as duke?"

"Ha! Not unless he needs someone with more sway in his little court. He still can't stand me, but who knows? Maybe we'll fuck and forget all about this."

"Oh, but you'll have to get through Baal."

Rosier stood where he was, eyes furrowed as Gemory's words echoed in his head.

"I'll fuck them both!" The crowd howled in laughter again. "Unless there's anyone here who wants to try stopping me?" For a brief moment, as Moloch spun around, and his face was pointed in the perfect direction, Rosier and the ex-duke's gazes met. Moloch quirked a brow at the same time a smirk twirled an end to his lips, but he said nothing; he was waiting, waiting for Rosier to be the one to speak.

A few times, Rosier blinked, but there was a knot in his throat twisting and twisting. He lowered his eyes, then followed the lead of the one who'd yelled at him, careful to breathe in and begin to walk away from all of this. There was a chuckle behind him — Moloch, sounding cruel, almost victorious. Trying not to listen, Rosier searched for daylight; like when he was young, he hurried for his fruits, thinking of laying against the trunk of an orchard tree, but he didn't feel like a newly-made heavenly creature no matter his actions. The more he walked, the more the truth sunk into his very blood that it would never feel the same to lay beneath the bright sky like when he was a few years old and unknowing of evil. He was not the same. His fruits had finally fallen with him, and there were orchards now, growing and growing. 'But it will not be like Heaven here.' Ever.

At the end of a corridor, the shine of the sun — a beady pearl growing wider with each step. 'This isn't paradise even if those I love most are here.' Rosier hadn't lied to Satan that he still carried so much love with him — but maybe he and Satan had been wrong about its nature. Maybe he wasn't a ghost of paradise. 'I cannot even imagine paradise anymore.' Maybe his love wasn't that of the angel Rosier who refused to die. It wasn't angel Rosier or demon Rosier; it was merely *Rosier*. The Rosier in between. Rosier could suffer a million deaths, but there were some things that would never change, that would remain with him. He couldn't change who he was, not even for the one he loved more than himself.

THE EIGHTH MEMORY

A smodeus tried to kill himself a few times, as an angel. On the first attempt, he did it without thinking, looking through the wooden crate of tools he'd been handed. All around him, there were trees, partly disembodied and tied to the rocky ground by their roots, whereas the firmament above was still shattered enough that there were fragments of a dark abyss with stars freckling through. There was no Earth yet; thus, there were no clouds, no gates of pearl. Heaven was nothing but pieces of what could become wholes but were, for now, only half-made branches, spores and not seeds, rock hills, and cosmic dust. The stone he was crouched over was cold on his feet, but the long, thin saw in his left grip was colder, especially as he lifted it to eye level. Behind him, his wings fluttered like leaves in breeze, neither which quite existed yet. "Hm." In the distance, there were some angels, gathered by the prince Uriel, who was perched on a towering rock. Staring at their naked bodies, Asmodeus raised the saw to his throat; the angels didn't wear clothes yet.

Chillingly, the teeth of the saw tapped at his skin, sinking in with a novel sort of pain that made Asmodeus flinch. His mouth fell open, and as he pressed deeper, the pressure on his vocal cords building and building, his mouth began to feel wetter, hotter.

Almost by accident, his arm jerked, the saw slicing his throat open jaggedly. A deluge of thick red stumbled down to his chest, and he loosened his grip on the tool, but it remained where it was lodged. Shocks of pain twitched his body, each move wrenching more blood up to his throat and to his mouth. Within seconds, he was seeing greater spots of dark above him, then falling onto him. 'Ow,' he finally thought as his left foot slipped beneath his weight, and he crashed onto his shoulder, legs kicking uselessly, wings erratically flapping against himself and the stone. 'That's all the pain I can handle.' He hadn't even realized he was curious to know, but it was a relief. A new sensation to behold. 'They're calling my name. Uriel will be so angry. He will say God is angry.'

Some other time — there was no time yet — Asmodeus met God, an instance that he'd been walking on the edge of a galaxy with some friends. He'd been laughing, shoving at them, until he'd noticed a bursting star at his peripheral — one of those spheres of flames that Uriel had told them some strange story about once. His gaze was drawn to it, and he walked along the tightrope of the universe's end, heading toward it and not waiting for the angels he'd been with to notice he'd slipped away. Just as Asmodeus thought of reaching out and pinching the faraway nova between two fingers, he heard a voice, on the other side of the edge of space — a person speaking from the other side of all things. Slowly, he turned his head, and he saw Him. The Lord. He didn't recognize such a thing to be a thing, didn't even make a shape out of Him, but Asmodeus knew that was the Creator, a being so heavy that if Asmodeus lost balance, he felt he'd be pulled in, fall into the hole, the gaping lightless maul of God's face.

"Lord," Asmodeus had said, face brightening in wonder. "My Father. Praise be to you, Father. Is this really you?" His heart swelling and swelling with love. "I've heard so much of you."

"Asmodeus."

"Thank you. What an honor to hear my name. How can I be of service?"

"Return to your brothers."

"Yes, Father." And he would try to never look to the stars again. "Thank you for them, as well. I'm happy to not be alone."

"It's no good for an angel to be alone, but do not ever turn your back on God in order to look at a friend."

Asmodeus lifted a foot, hearing now the voices of his friends shouting after him, and he dangled a leg past the edge, threatening to fall off the cosmos and plunge into God, into nothing, into death. His second suicide attempt. Had wings and the hands of the other angels not reached him, Asmodeus might've sunk into the darkness past the end. But touch saved him, the touch of his friends had saved him. From God, their Father. Yet, Asmodeus turned to his friends with his body tensed as if in panic and demanded to know why they stopped him. The angels all stared at him wildly, asking why he'd stood there and spoken to nothing. Nothing? It was a response that haunted Asmodeus for a while, one that he even asked Uriel about in a second he caught him alone.

Uriel replied: "If our Father is everything, then we can assume He may be nothing too." The prince of the angels drew orbital spheres with his index in newborn sand by a newborn sea in Heaven. "When we imagine *things*, we imagine an object that *is* by separating it from the objects that it *isn't*. If there is nothing that isn't God, then it's hard to imagine God as anything but *nothing*. Do you make sense of this? Are you listening to me, Asmodeus? Don't concern yourself too much with God's nature. You'll only annoy yourself. Take that saw and get to building. Don't mutilate yourself again."

"Why not?" Asmodeus asked, half in curiosity and half in jest. "With all this new water, healing will be much easier."

"Focus on building."

"Oh, brother, you never answer me. You must be the angel of impatience."

"If only you were the angel of focusing on building." And Uriel rose to his feet, turned around, wearing a thin garment like a tunic but tied oddly at the back. Uriel, for as much of a starch traditionalist as he was, had adopted clothing instantly, like it was the ailment to a pain he'd long suffered for. Naked, Asmodeus remained where he was, still crouching, his hair like twin dark rivers pouring down past both shoulders. Allegedly, God was pleased with clothing. And He was pleased with the city, had even walked the stony paths once, though Asmodeus had been asleep that day.

Many angels had found purposes now, knew what they were made for. Oddly, Asmodeus wasn't really interested to learn his own role among the angels, what gaps he was meant to fill. It was the only mystery in his life, he felt. If he answered it, then why continue living? He would like to enjoy not being committed to one thing. He wanted his attention everywhere. He wanted to be constructing himself forever, or else what would he do with all his time? 'God, do forgive me,' he thought with some shame, 'but I can be so bored in paradise.'

Billions of years later, Asmodeus tried to kill himself again, just because he'd had nothing better to do. He fought with another angel in a plaza, both of them clashing swords as the crowd around them beat their hands together and hollered. "Aren't you the angel of dueling?" Asmodeus had teased at his opponent, then grinned at everyone's laughter. "Go on," he baited him, "cut out my heart!" Those would be stupid words if he cared about avoiding pain, but Asmodeus was asking for it. After he was knocked to the ground, the dueler stabbed right through his chest, impaling his heart, then tore it out through his front to show the still-beating muscle skewered on the sword to the awed onlookers. Though he screamed, Asmodeus had wanted this. It was difficult to explain why, why the pain felt so good at times. Why it made him feel so *alive* when doing eight tasks at once to stimulate his mind wasn't doing enough.

But it was this suicide attempt that had brought him Raphael, who wasn't yet a prince. He broke through the crowd with a wooden staff and a pail of water from the sea — there wasn't yet a fountain, nor was there a center to Heaven — and hurried to Asmodeus' body jerking uselessly as he suffocated on the golden taste of his blood. "Brother," Raphael cried, "put your hands down." Asmodeus hadn't even realized they were raised, but in the blackness tinting his vision — like the sight of God — he saw flashes of the healer before him. His curved nose, his long lashes, his oak hair, and his blue eyes like the sea he carried in a wooden bucket — one of those angels that Asmodeus could label one of the most beautiful, the sort that made Asmodeus wish they never began to wear clothes in Heaven. "Stay still. I will help you. Please never do something so harmful again."

There was no point, no point in taking care of your body in the eternal city of pleasure, but not too much pleasure.

Asmodeus came to like Raphael, quite a bit. He saw him often. The prince, before he was a prince, always cleaned Asmodeus' wounds extensively and tenderly. He smiled gently at Asmodeus' dry jokes, and he had a handsome expression whenever he stared off and simply thought. "You're," Raphael once laughed with him, "not serious enough about anything, Asmodeus. You should be. Worshiping God involves praying more and being a good angel." After Raphael became an archangel, he still smiled, fond, at Asmodeus whenever he had to deal with his mishaps. He even once used Asmodeus as a model for another healing angel, Samyaza, to teach on the typical angel body.

Then, Asmodeus began to hurt himself on purpose, just to see Raphael again.

But the archangel realized it far too quickly; he noted how Asmodeus was jumping haphazardly into brawls, duels, and accidents that weren't much of accidents. Not mentioning it at first, Raphael nonetheless began to frown when they spoke and eventually sternly ordered Asmodeus to take better care of himself. "I'm exhausted," Raphael sighed at him. "I'm exhausted enough without you giving me more to do, Asmodeus." He had other things to do than take care of this single angel who didn't want to die but also really seemed to be trying to. "Please, give me some time, friend. I want to rest."

The cruel result of a hasty first crush — Asmodeus and Raphael began to grow apart, saw each other less often, had less to talk about when they could once converse for days without stopping. Feeling emptier, emptier, Asmodeus felt all hope lost, but he didn't know what he'd been hoping for. He'd given himself no purpose to live, willingly, but now he had nothing to dream for, no reason to get up from bed. His attachment to Raphael had been a burst of meaning, but he only realized it now, now that it was gone. Once angels began counting time, he only realized truly how much of his life had passed and how much more would. He looked to the future and saw nothing in it. Drinking, dancing, fighting, even all at once, could only do so much to alleviate the pain of being so conscious of eternity. Friendships were the only other thing he had, but however close he was to an angel, he craved more. He craved deeper. He craved.

'Angel of craving,' he told himself. 'Is that what I am, Father? Angel of craving?' He could only soothe himself with the thought that God must understand him. He knew all things. He was meaning just as much as He was meaningless.

There were a few more suicide attempts — random, disjointed. For some time, Asmodeus grew addicted to chariot racing, and before one match, he downed as many liquors as he could. He hoped to crash. He hoped to be run over by every angel in Heaven, just to know how much he could break, just to see the emptiness past the edge of the universe, to die and see God. God would understand him. God would listen.

Asmodeus received what he asked for: on the second lap around the stadium, his chariot tipped over, and he felt the sandy ground crash against him, so hard that his elbow immediately was pushed out of his skin, and his ankle twisted violently to one side. Distantly, there were gasps from the audience, horror and shock, but they paled in comparison to the yells that came when the chariot behind Asmodeus couldn't swerve around him in time.

The wheels rolled over his torso, dragging him through the ground, and crushing his abdomen so greatly that he felt his own intestines pushed up into his chest, into his throat, out of his mouth. His legs were also shredded, the bones in them flattened, the muscles that embraced them bursting as if they'd swelled and popped. It was some of the closest he'd come to death — pure darkness, blood in his ears blocking out all the noise, complete emptiness except for the unimaginable pain screaming from every point on his body.

Another chariot was headed toward him, but someone grabbed the mangled body of Asmodeus and yanked him out of the way a second before it could be further damaged. Cheers followed, as well as joyous drum beatings. Spottily, Asmodeus saw a soft face, dark skin, frazzled bangs, and long hair. His eyes were honey, his face was twisted in utter terror. The wings spread above provided Asmodeus a little shade from the permanent blaze of the firmament, and he tried to speak through the blood in his mouth, though he wasn't sure what he could possibly be saying.

'Who are you?' he wanted to ask. 'I'm Asmodeus. I've never seen you before, and I've seen everything. I've felt a thousand hands but none really like yours. A million eyes I've looked into but none really like yours.'

His name was Rosier; he was the angel of fruit. After Asmodeus was healed by Raphael and another healer — though they told him he would need to rest for some time because the water was upset to have to heal him once more — there were constant knocks at the door from him, this Rosier. The angel of fruit kept coming by, checking that Asmodeus was following orders to rest. Many times, Rosier would grab his sleeve and, stomping, drag Asmodeus up the stairs to the bedroom, only to then start tucking the old angel into bed. Quickly, he cut fruits for him, and he brushed the hair Asmodeus had allowed to knot, even preened his wings. He was excessively fussy, but it made Asmodeus smile. He liked him. He liked the way Rosier pretended not to like his jokes, too. He liked the way he rolled his eyes and tapped his head with rolled up parchment and struggled when Asmodeus embraced him in thanks only to soften and hug him back tighter. He liked that Rosier was the perfect height for him to rest his arm over his head.

"Take your hand off! Also, take better care of yourself. If I catch you being so careless with the knives again, I'll hit you with this pan."

"So I'd end up hurt regardless?"

"Yes, and I'll be upset. Do you want that?"

"Hmm."

"Say no."

"Alright. I suppose I don't want to upset you, sweet Rosier."

Huffing — "Good!"

He decided he couldn't attempt suicide again any time soon, or else he'd upset Rosier. And, another day, he started nagging the angel of fruit to move in, and Asmodeus built a room on the first floor that he thought would suit him. For good measure, he took some fruit trees from a few willing orchards and made them a patio to live and breathe in. He was happy, even happier when Rosier saw the surprise and lit up like he never had. Curling up to rest together, afterward, Asmodeus's face hurt from smiling so much. For all of eternity up to this point, Asmodeus had tried to run away from a purpose to live, but it seemed God had sent it to him directly, now, in the shape of an angel named Rosier.

CHAPTER 10

Opening the door, tepid and slow, Rosier arrived home; it was nighttime now, though he didn't know it. His hand remained on the wooden paneling as he held his gaze on the only glow in the room, in a corner where the light of the corridors behind Rosier didn't reach. A figure was hunched over, the end of a blunt in his mouth whereas the other tip was lit enough to illuminate some of an angelic, beautiful face. Turning up his head, the creature revealed anxious eyes at Rosier, as well as an open robe, loosely tied at the waist, and something squirming in his hands, over crossed legs. Asmodeus took his blunt and ground it against the stone ground, his mouth opening wide to speak, but Rosier did it first. He saw the animal against Asmodeus' claws — a four-legged, furred rodent with a wispy tail — and whispered, "Oh? How did he get in here?"

"He's pregnant," Asmodeus said simply; there was no other pronoun than the one they both knew. "But, Rosier, where—" His voice was small, uncharacteristically fragile and hushed, almost frightened. "Where have you been?" Though he was moving to act, to grimace and stand up, Rosier was quicker once again. Shutting the door, dousing them both in near darkness, save for the cracks in the wooden panels — the fallen angel of fruit crossed the room over to Asmodeus and lowered to his knees beside him. His hand lifted to hover over the small head of the rodent. "Rosier—"

"Oh, he's so upset," Rosier said about her sniveling snout, then smiled, his gaze soft. "Did your other half leave you all alone like this? We will find and punish him for you." But the rodent didn't reply, and Asmodeus held her a little closer as he leaned toward Rosier with curved, worried brows. Rosier couldn't ignore it, couldn't stop from meeting Asmodeus' eyes, feeling his smile turn sadder but remain on his face nonetheless. "Hello..."

"Where have you been?"

"I'm sorry. I didn't mean to scare you." Rosier breathed in, lowering the hand he'd raised to settle it right beside one of Asmodeus' feet, something taken from an ancient beast and shaped like the claws of a rooster. "I was with Lucifer. I needed to get away from you. Just for some time." He didn't miss how a shadow of pain passed over Asmodeus' face, and Rosier felt some of his own heart sting to know he might be hurting his friend, but he had hurt Asmodeus many times already. He butchered him often, and Asmodeus had hurt him. Had butchered him too. "I discovered something horrible, but it's true. It's a horrible truth. I learned that there are some parts of me that I can't change. There are some parts of me that I have no choice but to carry and that no amount of demons or even the devil can do away with. Not even you, not even my love for you can change some of me." His voice was somber, but it wasn't shaking, like he was finding more relief in this than pain, despite the burn.

"What's wrong, Rosier?" Asmodeus stroked a gentle thumb against the head of the rodent. "I don't want you to run away without informing anyone. If you're going to leave forever, at least tell me so that I know you're safe."

"Would you chase after me if I left?"

"I don't want to hurt you."

"You've already hurt me."

"I'm sorry." Asmodeus sighed harshly, then shook his head and shifted. "Fuck. I'm sorry for everything."

Rosier said, "What's the difference between being hurt once or a thousand times by you? I thought there was none, but I see now that there is. It never stops hurting." He finally settled to plop down beside Asmodeus. "When I try to imagine leaving this place, I can't see anything. It was the same way I felt of Heaven. There are places that I feel I belong to, even if they are no good for me. I fear you're no good for me either. But I can't imagine anywhere but here, or maybe I don't want to. I chose to fall, and I stand by that decision. Paradise is not paradise, and my friend is not my friend. He's something else." He stared at Asmodeus' shameful, avoiding eyes. "The worst part is that I think we love each other."

"I do love you," Asmodeus whispered. "God, I do."

"God?"

"Rosier, I do."

"I don't want to be God."

Asmodeus turned a bittersweet smile to him. "Do you think God decided to be God? We make gods out of those who want it or not. And if you choose to never speak to me again, I'll still pray to you. I'll hope to hear from you again but only to know you're happy."

Rosier hesitated, then confessed, "I don't like fucking." It was one of the few times he'd uttered the word out loud, and it almost hurt to say, like he was tearing free the last shred of angelic innocence he'd so dearly held to his heart. When Asmodeus grimaced again, he continued, "I had to be half-aware to do it or else it would feel like little more than discomfort and dirtiness. There were a few times I did like it, but they weren't often. Sometimes, I told you to continue even if I didn't want it."

Asmodeus murmured, "There were times when I wasn't certain. I'm sorry."

Rosier ignored him; he wasn't God, he didn't take apologies. "I began to miss the time when you took on other lovers and did nothing but kiss and hold me. Even still, I kept allowing you to fuck me. I thought that if I did it enough, I would begin to fully enjoy it, but that's never come. Yesterday, I realized how much pain I was in, how much I had attempted to numb myself because I wanted you to love me how you wanted."

"Forgive me."

"*No*," Rosier said, his throat beginning to burn, his teeth clenching. "No, I won't forgive you." He shut his eyes, and he tried to find something to ground him in the darkness, but it was a sea of black, and he was sinking. "I don't want to, but— But— There is no other place for me. I'm going to be in this cave until God burns us all up. I made that decision. I am a demon no matter how I act. I chose this place, and I chose not to ask for forgiveness in Heaven. I won't choose forgiveness now either." He tried to breathe; it was clumsy, short. "All I want is to not hurt any more than I have to."

"I'll never do it with you again," Asmodeus promised hastily. "I never want to hurt you—"

"What I *want*," Rosier interjected, "is for us to love one another and to find a way to be happy. Before we burn. That's all I want. I want to be as happy as I can with you. I want a taste of Heaven again. How it was in Heaven between us but with a little more, just some extra kisses and touching. I'm not like the others, Asmodeus. You can do what you want with the others, but I'm not like them." His eyes opened again, slow. 'Can you love me more than you want to fuck me?'

The demon of lust answered: "You've always been different to me. It's why I loved you. And it's why I'll keep loving you, Rosier."

At that, the fallen angel of fruit could only smile happily, sadly, wonderfully, and painfully; he put a hand over Asmodeus', his fingers on the talons that cradled the small rodent. "Love is all I can ask for." 'Because I know better.' There was never going to be a better; this was the life he'd chosen, or rather the death he'd chosen. He should even be grateful for the pain he suffered now, because one day, it would only be the pain of burning that he knew. The fires at the end of their rebellion. God's punishment. "But I was struggling to be happy with what we were doing. I tried. I hope you're not angry." A part of him wanted to say that he hoped Asmodeus would forgive him, but there was something terribly tired in him, too exhausted to apologize. Or maybe he didn't want to apologize at all. Maybe he'd done nothing that he needed to ask forgiveness for.

"Of course not— I could never be angry at you—"

"Can I," Rosier cut in, "know where you found this poor creature?" He was tired of this conversation.

Silence. Asmodeus hesitated, face still set in deep worry, until the animal in his hands began to stir again, squeaking and curling her tail. Quiet, he explained, "I found him by one of the entrances; one of his legs is sprained. I was looking for you, and I wasn't planning to come back until I learned where you were, but — I just thought he was interesting. Some animals have eggs, most of them do, but there are a lot now that hold their offspring inside their own bodies." He shifted, then he looked at Rosier and added, "One time, I was talking with demons about offspring. I don't like the idea of it, personally. And, look, this little thing seems so weak. It's curious, but it's miserable to watch."

"I'm glad you brought him in," said Rosier, laying his head on Asmodeus' shoulder, staring at the rodent turning her small head up at them, her belly round and, in some sense, unwieldy. "We should take care of him."

Asmodeus said, "I think we should, as well." He turned, his lips pressing against the fallen angel of fruit's cheek, and when Rosier turned his face to him, their mouths met in a tender peck. "I'll do anything you ask me, darling Rosier. Are you well? You should rest."

"Not yet..." Rosier nuzzled his own mouth against Asmodeus' in a loving gesture. "Should I light a fire? Then, I can try to make a nest of blankets for him. And you — does anything hurt?"

"Nothing that needs immediate attention. I'll help you with the nest, and I'll give him a fruit. I have one; I always keep one for emergencies."

"What? Why?"

"In case you need it. And, look, now we need it. I'm very wise at times, Rosier."

Rosier paused, then laughed softly. "Help me with the fire and think what you want."

They didn't fuck, not when they ate with the mammal or afterward. They didn't even do it once they were getting ready for bed. Even stranger, they kissed without Asmodeus instantly grinding against him. With their bodies tangled after a day of such stress, their lips met once again in slow, chaste movements. There was some rousing, a familiar stiffness growing to press against one of Rosier's thighs, but Asmodeus turned away the lower half of himself, and Rosier felt sin's touch leave him, just its ghost and memory remaining on his body. A soft breath, almost tasting of relief, skittered from the younger one's mouth, but there was a pang of guilt. There would always be. There would always be guilt, wouldn't there?

Sleep crept onto him, and Rosier dreamt of nothing.

For the next few days, the two offered the rodent a great deal of their attention. Rosier collected a healthy mix of greenery and meat for her, and he was happy to introduce her to fruits, to talk with her and comfort her through spells of nausea and general discomfort. He stroked her little body and listened to the responding squeaks with a smile. Out in the hallways, he saw demons look at him, glower at him. He ignored it. There were other things to do. With the rodent in a sling like he used to carry a decapitated friend, he headed out from the caves, visited the orchard that had once been a meadow. The uneven and jagged rows of trees towered around him; their fruits always fell onto his open hands, and it was easy to feel himself again. To find himself, too — this new Rosier on Earth. A place that glimmered a slow-moving clockwork of stars above each evening, a place overbrimming with singing life. A creature that was bearing more life was curled up against his front, and Rosier was not an angel anymore. He was in a place like Heaven that was, maybe, better — in some ways at least. He was in a paradise again, if he allowed it to be.

"We're all going to die," Rosier told the rat, and that was becoming easier to say. "But we're going to be happy until then. Us demons and you animals. We're going to find happiness here." Or die in the trying. "I promise that life will get better for you. For the both of us." He kissed her head and listened to the breeze whistling through the branches and climbing up into the coming sunset, blanketing the sky in steaks of orange and pink. "You may even be lucky that the animal who left you in this state is gone." He wasn't sure what he meant by that, so he decided to end his speaking and enjoy the silence with the rat. She didn't speak much, perhaps found the demons were too frightening. 'Am I frightening to you, also? Even without horns on my head or a tail sweeping the air behind me?'

"Rosier?"

Like he'd been physically pulled, Rosier's body jumped and turned. His eyes were wide, his lips slightly parted, his gaze landing on, first, the one who'd spoken — a large demon with hefty horns — then the beautiful devil standing a step behind, half hidden behind the manufactured bulk of their old friend. "Baal," left Rosier's mouth, quiet. He wasn't sure that he'd ever seen Baal here before, but he remembered the day Asmodeus had tasted a peach for the first time since the fall, how he'd kissed, then held, then fucked Rosier around here. Would Asmodeus and him never be intimate again that way? "Forgive me." In his arms, the rodent began to squirm. "I've been here with this animal for too long. I hope I'm not in the way of either of you."

Quick, Baal shook his head. "Oh, not really. Lucifer said he wanted to talk to me, but we weren't going anywhere."

Lucifer spoke with a level voice, without a particular tone or hint of feeling: "What is that animal?" He stepped around Baal, some of his hair fluttered by breeze, then moved toward Rosier, but the fallen fruit angel adjusted the cloth around the rodent, covering her body. "It's too small to be butchered for any of Asmodeus' needs." He was as beautiful as he had been in bed, his lips as soft-looking as they'd felt against Rosier's mouth.

"He's not," Rosier cut in, "for any butchering." His brow furrowed. "I'm just caring for him while he's... unwell."

"Hm," said the devil, tilting his head and peering down. "Oh, pregnant. I see. It should give birth soon. Careful, there's typically blood." He lifted a hand, but he didn't touch the rodent who lifted her face, instead merely holding his palm over her like he were blessing the coming child. "Well." And he lowered his hand again. "I suppose it's good that we've stumbled upon you. I was about to tell Baal that Moloch is causing trouble again. He tried to have Gemory gang-raped after they argued publicly. I'm running out of patience."

Baal was crossing his arms and grumbling. "Are you worried Gemory will make a bigger problem out of this? I say we should let them fight."

"I don't like," Satan said, "when a demon who is not a duke commands others in our caves. At the same time, I can't banish him. If I do, he'll antagonize me and build an army of the demons wandering the Earth. And you, Baal," he added sharply, "are you perfectly content with a demon like him, who thinks he can order even you around? You'll be his next victim, and then you'll cry to me after he's had you tied and bent over a rock for all his friends to enjoy." Baal's face fell into a glower, his mouth twitching to reveal a hint of his sharpened teeth. "So, something must be done, and I wanted to hear from the dukes. I know what I can't do: I can't punish him again, at least not so directly, or he'll resent me. His resentment will spread to other demons, and it will create division. I have to alter my approach."

Rosier glanced down at the mammal in his hold, at her sniveling nose. 'Poor Gemory asked me to do something, didn't he?' But he had done nothing. ' Though I couldn't have stopped Moloch, surely. Of course not.' He swallowed. 'I don't want to know if I could have.' The rodent nuzzled his fingers, the minuscule pink tongue peeking out to lap at his skin. 'But I do know how many animals I've butchered, even if I'm holding this one so gently now.'

"Alter how?" Baal asked.

"As much as I enjoy to be feared, it was fear of God that created our rebellion in Heaven. I must ensure that Moloch continues to adore me, that his fear for me never trumps his worship." In a second of silence, animals in the forestry called and cooed. "That is where I need the dukes to help me." Satan interlocked his hands before his front, then offered Baal and Rosier a pleasant, sugary smile. "You must punish him, and you must find a way to lead Moloch's friends away from him. Once he's frustrated and isolated, I'll invite him to my bed." Baal made a low, dissatisfied grunt. "In his lowest moment, I'll bring him comfort, and I will be all he loves for a time. He'll never want to let go of me after that, and he will listen to me."

Rosier adjusted the sling that was against his front, his features scrunched in worry, in dislike. He had allowed someone to be hurt, but he didn't know if he could bring himself to hurt someone himself. Beside him, Baal was answering, "I can try to punish him, maybe have him humiliated somehow."

"You'll have to plan this well or else you'll be the one who gets embarrassed and shamed," Satan warned, though with a touch of amusement.

Rosier had made up his mind about the type of person he was, or at least he was hoping so. "Lucifer?" he called, not missing how Satan's eyes gleamed with near excitement when they turned to him. "I can't do this." Rosier shook his head, then he staggered away. "Forgive me."

"You can't do what?" But Rosier took some steps past Satan and Baal. "What is it you can't do, Rosier?"

Rosier listened to the squeaks of the rodent, pitched in terror.

"I can't be a duke, Satan." He walked a little more but wasn't able to resist turning back, seeing the hardened face of the devil and the tilted head of Baal. "Please do forgive me." He wanted to say, 'This is the least I could do, isn't it? To do less harm?' Or was he just running from authority?

Satan told him, "There's no choice for you."

"I won't call myself a duke. I won't respond to it. And no one has ever really seen me as such." Again, the animals in the forest were singing. "There are plenty of others who will be more helpful to you than me. Consider Asmodeus." He knew he shouldn't have said that, but Lucifer didn't physically react; even still, Rosier could sense the anger in the pit of his friend's belly. "Again, forgive me."

"Rosier," Baal tried, but the fallen angel of fruit held the rodent tight then spun on his heel and hurried away.

CHAPTER 11

Within a few months, Asmodeus was coming home, again, smelling of sex. One should suppose this was to be expected. Rosier hadn't made a request of complete celibacy; it hadn't crossed his mind to ask for. Thus, Rosier wasn't sad, really. His melancholy was like nostalgia when he woke to Asmodeus holding him — though the lustful one had been missing the night before — with the familiar sin-stench on him. Such a smell was no longer a stranger to their bed as it had been the first time Asmodeus returned to him that way. Breathing slow, turning his head, Rosier's nose bumped against Asmodeus', and he watched a smile bloom over the mouth of his friend. Drowsily, the demon of lust leaned forward, stealing a morning kiss. "I hope," Rosier whispered, eyes itching, "last night went well. Are you... tired?" Nearby, a litter of rats was squeaking over a bundle of cloth.

"Mm, sorry, should I wash? Yes, I'm tired, but I don't really want to talk of that when I'm with you. I know that you don't like to hear about it, and I care nothing for those demons I fuck. Once I've finished, I have nothing to say about it. There's nothing attached to it, no feelings." He said it again, firmer, "They mean *nothing* to me." He was trying to reassure him.

Maybe there was nothing to do now but wait until Asmodeus decided that his lust was greater than his love. He would stop returning to bed with Rosier one of these days, surely. He would begin to hug someone else, stop speaking to Rosier as often, as tenderly. He would come to kiss him less; one day, their lips would meet for the final time. This, Rosier was certain of. 'He will even stop considering me a friend, one day, won't he? He'll see me as a mistake he made multiple times. Something he broke and was unable to fix.' On the rare mornings when Asmodeus was gone, maybe having left to find them something to eat or to gather something for his pain, Rosier would lift a hand and stretch it toward the cave ceiling, staring at his fingers, his fallen angel hands, and he would think of taking the sun in his grip, that bright sphere like an orange. 'One day, I will be just another memory to you, won't I?' Asmodeus.

'But you will never be a memory to me. I think that I'll always carry an ever-present, beating heart of you. My hands will never lose the feeling of yours. Your weight will forever press down on me. Your body. My mouth is going to taste of you forever.' Even as his lips laid on someone else. 'Your blood is still hot on my skin. One day, it will begin to burn. Forever.'

Asmodeus always returned, however, and if Rosier's hand was still raised, he'd take it, his claws slipping in between the fingers. Demon hand and Rosier's hand, which was no longer that of an angel no matter how many flowers he might put in his hair or the fruits he might carry. Sweetly, Asmodeus nuzzled him. Here Rosier was, thinking of how much he'd spend the rest of eternity grieving once Asmodeus left him for a better lover, while Asmodeus embraced him in utter adoration, not letting go. No matter how much he should. "Rosier, Rosier. Darling Rosier." The fallen angel of fruit leaned into all the affection, the peppering kisses all over his cheeks and nose and eyelids.

There was a foul part of him that was happy he'd marked Asmodeus' body forever, and an even fouler part hoped that only he might be able to recreate him no matter who

Asmodeus eventually left him for. But, the feeling immediately saddened him, and the voice of Gemory echoed in his mind, as it occasionally did. He was no better than the others. They were all wicked, even the kindest things in the world were wicked.

After yet some more months of the same, there was another festival, this one dedicated to a brisk, lovely autumn. Rosier was not at all involved with this one, hadn't even been consulted or had the chance to labor the day of as had been the case with the first summer solstice festival. Confirmation, perhaps, that Lucifer was relieving him of duty, maybe even considering Rosier's recommendation of Asmodeus, which Baal seemed a big proponent of.

Rosier, anyway, went for some figs and returned with a heavy basket of them an hour or two before the beginning of the celebration. As he was heading back to his room, he heard a voice, vaguely familiar but certainly not that of a friend, saying — "Asmodeus, that piece of shit Asmodeus." Like an alerted lovebird, Rosier twisted his head in the direction of the speaker, encountering two demons seated on a bench beside a jagged, short tunnel in the cave, the beginnings of a new hallway; in between them, there was a simple, prototypical hookah, and in their hands they each held something of a pipe. "He nearly pulled my hair out," the demon continued, face cringing in flickers of shame, anger. "He almost tore open my throat. There's never been a more selfish lover." Cold, colder — Rosier's blood ran through him, and he put one foot before the other, walking faster.

"He frightened you?" asked the demon's friend.

"He did," responded the conflicted one. "But there's something even more terrible about Asmodeus. He hurts you, then you crawl back to him. He makes you believe he'll change. He doesn't. And it becomes hard to tell what's good and what's painful with him. You can't help but worry what he can turn you into— Oh, a masochist!" Rosier was so far now that the voices were muffled, but he still heard that dreadful word again. "That is what he wants, a masochist!"

Tightening his grip on the basket, there was a hollowness in the fallen angel of fruit's head and his heart. An unwillingness to think about what he'd heard. Instead, he focused on finding the door to the chamber he shared with that frightening demon the others were talking about. He stepped inside, pulling the door closed behind him, and looked over at Asmodeus sitting at the edge of the bed, offering a minuscule piece of meat to two little rodents sitting on a beastly knee. He wore a heavy robe, embroidered in earthly colors. Long, dark hair fell past both shoulders like rivers of onyx, some ribbons creating scattered, tiny braids among it. His tail was by his feet, curling around a bony ankle, and there was some jewelry dangling from his horns, the ends of the chains occasionally brushing at a face that was painted darkly by the eyes and reddish at the lips, lips that were curling up into a smile as Rosier flushed.

"Hello," greeted the demon.

"Oh, you're already dressed. I just thought to go for some figs before the festivities began, but I'll try to hurry and dress too." Rosier hastily went to set the basket down by the trunk where he'd laid the tunic he planned to wear on top. It was also embroidered, and there were designs along it that had been by his own hand, whereas some other parts were carefully done by Asmodeus. "I walked past the field where Lucifer has prepared everything, and it's beautiful. If you want to go on ahead, please do." He'd already nearly forgotten about what he'd heard in the hall, and he was still entranced by the sight of his dear friend sitting there. Very rarely did Rosier feel anything other than shame when he saw the body he'd made for Asmodeus, but it'd seemed almost beautiful, for a second. Something abstract, made of pain but also love, some kind of art. Rosier could, very briefly, see how God could feel pride even at creating a monster.

"No, no," Asmodeus replied, "I'll wait. I'm... struggling with one of my hands. I brought a replacement if you'd like to help stitch it on, but it may be too large for the wrist." Rosier listened to the squeaks of the mother rodent on her cushion to his left as he pulled off his clothes, then reached for the ones he'd prepared. "But if it doesn't work, then I suppose it's no problem. I would just prefer to have two hands." Rosier nodded quickly, tugging his new tunic into place, then tying the strings on the garment over his chest to keep it from falling open. "My feet are not... doing too well either. I can't walk much." Rosier, too, pulled on some sandals of animal skin, thinking of what had died to decorate his body, then reached for his jewels. "But I'll do my best to dance with you." All that remained were the flowers for his hair, but as he attempted to stand before their mirror, to lay a crown of orange petals, Rosier noticed how empty his head looked 'without horns.'

"Don't," Rosier said quietly, "worry. There's no need to dance anyway." Though he knew Asmodeus did like to dance. "Let me help you with that hand." He smoothed his tunic and leaned over to kiss the mother rodent's head before rising back to his feet. Crossing the room toward his friend, he saw a disembodied, curled hand leaning against his thigh. "Oh." It was clawed, its skin rough. "I think it'll work." Asmodeus breathed out some gracious words, the rodents on his lap making high noises at them before they jumped onto the mattress, skittering along it and heading toward their mother.

"Mm, Rosier, you look very nice."

"Don't distract me." But Rosier smiled a little before going for the threads he used for stitches.

"Let me paint your face, darling, before we go."

"Hm."

"I beg you."

"Beg me after I finish with this."

Removing Asmodeus' bad hand was simple, and Rosier had gotten skilled enough at it that he no longer spilled as much blood, and though the new one took some trouble — it was indeed a little large but not overly so — it was soon attached with sturdy stitching. Asmodeus murmured that he had no feeling in it, though he could curl it in a fist well enough. "It'll do," he said, "for now. We'll see how long it lasts me." Then, he got his wish: Rosier sat and allowed his friend to paint his face with dark accents by the eyes and mouth, and Asmodeus added more jewelry to him too. Rosier didn't mind. He liked looking nice and Asmodeus' adoring eyes made him feel even nicer.

Together, they stepped out to wander the halls once they were done fixing each other up, their hands held, talons between fingers. There were some demons who saw, turned to one another and made comments, and there were some who joked right at them, asking if they'd just fucked and were feeling affectionate. But someone hissed at his friend: "No, they don't fuck — those two. Never have. That's the demon of lust and that's the demon of prude. The prude one thinks he's still an angel and that he's so much better than us. Asmodeus has been tricked." Tricked by his love.

The demon of lust and the demon of love. 'Both poisonous in excess, right?'

Past the cave's mouth, the two continued into the forestry, hearing already the signs of the festival before they reached it. Music — drums beating and timbrels whistling — and in between all the chatter and cries of pleasure — there were feet pounding the Earth they'd been damned to in dance. Asmodeus and Rosier approached and found, in between two especially tall trees, all that they'd expected: tables and cushions over a meadow like those of the first ever seasonal festival, with steaming foods and oils prepared in advance. Alcohol was passed around in chalices and bottles, new wine that Rosier had accidentally, indirectly, bore. The sun was setting, but only with its toes dipped into the horizon, so all the stars remained obscured by blue turning orange, hiding the hints of starry dark beginning to bleed through. And there was, of course, an orgy.

Demons were coupling on the ground, over flowers and over dirt they fisted their hands into, many using cushions but plenty of others not bothering. Their jewelry rattled as hips thrust, or as bodies twisted, creating a sort of rhythm for the musicians in their corners to follow, singing alongside the moans and whines. But not all of the festival was depravity; Rosier turned to his left and saw some demons discussing things, Lucifer among them, with an altar near to them of animal carcasses, particularly severed heads and hands. Some tails. "Oh," breathed the fallen angel of fruit and perhaps a blooming demon of unconditional love. 'They're getting new horns or changing their tails. I remember Gemory said the horns and tails help to balance. Horns are trophies of the bravery we had to fall.' Rosier walked his gaze back to Asmodeus, who had his eyes on the orgy, and only then did he realize how firm his friend was squeezing his hand, only narrowly not slicing off any fingers with his claws. "You can go."

Asmodeus shook his head, turning to Rosier, his mouth opening, then stammering, "I'd rather be with you."

"Go," Rosier insisted, snaking his hand away from Asmodeus' deathly grip. "I want to go... do something anyway. So, please don't worry. Go and enjoy yourself, Asmodeus. I know you want to." He gave him a smile, soft, but it wasn't so forced. A part of him was frightened, but he wasn't sad this time. That was all he could ask for. "I'll be back in an hour or so." He took the first steps, and the initial ones were heavy, but as he turned away from Asmodeus, had gained adequate distance, and his gaze focused on the devil, Rosier was walking easier, easier. When the eyes of Satan fell onto Rosier, he stopped conversing with two demons abruptly and tilted his head. There was a moment of nothing, no expression on Satan's face, no hint of joy or anger, until there was a smile. It wasn't much of a smile, partly hollow as always, but its pleasure twirled up to his eyes.

"Rosier," he greeted. "Have you come for some horns?"

The process was much shorter than anticipated; it was not even so painful, at least not in comparison to anything Rosier had felt these past few years, these past hundreds of thousand on Earth. He remembered believing, in Heaven, that pain was good;

it made one stronger. He was learning that lesson again, through Lucifer's touch, his perfect hands stitching and searing horns to Rosier's skull how the demon of fruit had added a new hand to Asmodeus' wrist. For now, there would be no tail; it would take some more time before Rosier could live with re-creating himself any further. But his new horns were curled like a ram's, and they greatly complemented his head shape, as Lucifer had promised. The devil even placed a hand mirror before the face of Rosier, who was sat over a cushion, and showed him the result after wiping at the blood that'd dribbled past his ears. Rosier saw his face, he saw himself. His head was heavy but not in an unfamiliar way; it reminded him of the weight of his old hair, thick and long.

This demon, this corpse of angel Rosier, would learn to be happier here. 'I will be. I will be.' He smiled, his eyes so fragile he might break. 'I will be.' And he would. With a kiss to the edge of his mouth, Satan told Rosier to go join the others, his hand giving Rosier's shoulder a light, affectionate squeeze. Rosier kissed his cheek in return, then obeyed.

On his way back, he had no issue looking for and finding Asmodeus. There was a tall, beastly demon that had just finished with two others, who was sitting and shakily clutching his staff and grunting in pain or, perhaps, the remnants of release. Asmodeus, his hair in nearly as much disarray as his clothing, didn't notice Rosier coming up to his side. Instead, he continued drinking from a long bottle, shoving away his last fuck, almost aggressively, then murmured, "Give me a moment," as Rosier stepped up beside him. "I'm recovering. Don't come near me."

"Asmodeus."

Then, the lustful one startled, jerked his head to the side, his eyes widened so much they might escape his skull. "Rosier—" He stared. "You have... horns."

Rosier replied, "I do." Then, he leaned to Asmodeus's level and kissed his cheekbone. "I hope you don't mind them."

"No," was the hasty response. "They look nice. You look very good with them."

"I'm glad." When Asmodeus seemed to grimace again, Rosier felt himself frown, and he asked, quietly, "Do you want to leave the festival for a moment? Just so that you can recover however much you can? We can also return to our room."

Asmodeus replied, "Let's disappear into the forest for a moment. And then I'll decide." He laughed a little. "Though I would like to leave before Lucifer begins his usual speeches." He took a stronger, more ambitious grasp of his walking stick, then he rose to his feet, wobbling so much that Rosier instantly planted his hands on Asmodeus' torso, one palm up at his ribs and one by his lean stomach, and he thought of tilting his head and leaning his face against Asmodeus' chest for a second, listening to the rot inside him. Instead, he felt as Asmodeus readjusted himself, chuckling warmly, fondly. "Come. I know you don't like the loudness here either, friend." It was a very simple, considerate sentence, but it made Rosier's face warm, and he linked Asmodeus' free arm with his own and began walking.

The words of earlier returned to him — all the talk that the demon Asmodeus was a self-centered monster to his other lovers. He tricked them, then hurt them, then tricked them again. But Rosier was sure, or at least convinced, that Asmodeus was sincere with him. They had known each other too long for their relationship to be anything other than genuine. Maybe someone could be more than one thing, could be loving to some and a monster to others. The sounds of the festival grew dimmer, and the stars above brighter, as they trekked slowly down a hill toward the sound of rushing water. There was a river nearby; both of them had passed by it several times, but on their own. This was the first time they visited it together, at least Rosier believed so. If they'd sat at the riverbank with each other before, he didn't remember. Life is so long; how can anyone be expected to remember even the most important moments?

But nonetheless, they settled there, over each of the hard, colored pebbles. Asmodeus laid his head on Rosier's shoulder and the younger one smiled, reaching up to run his fingers through his friend's hair and feeling Asmodeus' horns brush him. Rosier was beginning to feel more comfortable with this all, with his own body as much as Asmodeus'. He dipped a foot into the water, the current rushing past perfectly cool; it was the sort of brisk sensation that could rouse you from sleep. Asmodeus whispered against him, "I love you." Rosier breathed in the autumn air, hearing the noises around them of animals, those who'd survived God's wrath and those who had been born from it.

"I love you too," the fruit demon sighed, taking Asmodeus' arm and tugging at it, wanting his friend to look at him, even if he didn't particularly want to look back. When Asmodeus lifted his head, turning his face to Rosier's, he leaned forward, pecked his lips against him. Rosier was relieved to shut his eyes. The smell of sex was heavy on Asmodeus, drowning them both, as Rosier pressed into the kiss, carving it deeper. Wrapping itself around him, Asmodeus' arm squeezed Rosier with a doting touch rather than a possessive one. Asmodeus's mouth dragged toward an edge of Rosier's, then he kissed along his jaw, his shivering throat. Rosier allowed it and felt Asmodeus curiously nuzzle at the tiny string bow of his tunic over his collarbone. "Mm."

"I'm sorry," Asmodeus said against him. "I'll stop if you want me to."

Rosier thought of how Asmodeus probably never said that to his lovers. "It's alright." Did the demon of lust reserve all his gentle touches and love for him? "I don't mind... today." He ran his fingers through Asmodeus' hair, again, twirling some of the little braids in it.

"Can I put my mouth on you?"

"Maybe." Rosier wasn't particularly aroused; he never was. But he liked this closeness. The memory of those years when fucking was all they'd done was mostly miserable, but he'd enjoyed some of the intimacy, some of the sweet love that Asmodeus could shower on him. So he allowed Asmodeus to mouth at his neck some more, to pull up on his tunic until it was up to his waist. "Ah," he gasped when Asmodeus' better hand gripped his inner thigh, his talons damp from having rested against the riverbed. "Don't," Rosier said softly, "put yourself in me. I don't want that."

"Of course," said Asmodeus, voice careful. "Whatever you wish. Would my tongue be too much?"

"I wouldn't mind it — your tongue." Rosier opened his eyes for a moment, watching as Asmodeus crawled back, began lowering his head toward the younger demon's groin.

"Only this," Rosier said, his voice so quiet he almost didn't hear himself, his hips twitching at the first sign of hot breath lapping at him, the tongue running up and swirling. "That feels good." Asmodeus asked if he was sure. "I can never be." But, for the third time, he put a hand in Asmodeus' hair, a shudder running up his spine and making — "Mmm," — a strangled moan escape. "Nothing more... than this, please." He wasn't even sure that he liked this, though it certainly wasn't awful either. The feeling was oddly neutral, not good *or* bad — and perhaps that was what demonhood was about. Rosier decided he might allow for touching like this, on a rare occasion. He could bear this, could even *enjoy* it. Once in a season.

One thing that Rosier knew he liked, though, was Asmodeus' muffled noises of worship, of praise. They were gentle, patient, even with his mouth *full* and grunting in need. He wasn't at all frightening the way his lovers spoke of. There must truly be some foulness in Rosier, then, even if he shrouded it in love; he knew how Asmodeus treated his lovers, had even seen it. And yet here he was, pulling on Asmodeus and thinking of letting him choke. The demon of lust adored him. Rosier was his favorite. The other demons were whores, but Rosier was the beloved. The others were concubines, but Rosier was the spouse. His heart scolded him for that moment of wickedness: 'How dare I decide to look away from what my friend does because I love him? How dare I?' But his gasps overcame him. Soon, he had lost control of his hips, even as Asmodeus' gripped them with both hands, and when Rosier finished, he saw each of the stars above, night having reached them, each spec of faraway light bearing witness.

"I love you," Rosier said, still trembling. "Too much." 'What have I done?' His love would kill him. His kindness churning his insides. Maybe there was such thing as too much kindness. Too much forgiveness, too much patience; he would offer too much. His loved ones would commit atrocities, and he would comfort them as they lay tired from their sins. He would clean the wounds of murderers merely because they were the friends he'd promised unconditional love to. He would stand aside and watch it happen. He was no better than them. For there are two kinds of devils — those who kill and those who knowingly welcome the killers home.

"I love you even more than that," Asmodeus told Rosier, crawling back over him, kissing him. "Believe me, I do. I'll do anything you ask." A few droplets spilled into Rosier's mouth in between the gentle kiss; he tasted himself; he tasted his own sin. "I'll kill anything you ask me to." 'But would you *not* kill, if I asked you to?' Rosier feared that he would never ask that, and he embraced him. Over the riverbed, the two remained for a while, a pair of tangled bodies partly-recreated.

They did, though, eventually return to the festival. When they did, there were some more upbeat songs playing and more food had been set on tables. Torches had been lit to cast a wide illuminating net over all the demons, and when Rosier saw some dancing at the center, he noticed their grins, their laughter. Instantly, he tugged Asmodeus by his robes, saying, "Do you think we can try dancing?" His friend laughed but heartily, lovingly. "Answer me."

"Yes. Yes, Rosier. As you wish." Asmodeus limped along with his staff, but he was quick, seemingly excited.

The demon of fruit snorted before he could help it, and the two snaked into the crowd. Taking Asmodeus' free hand, Rosier spun beneath it. He'd never been much of a dancer, always thought himself too tense, but he found it freeing now, and for once, everyone seemed too distracted to tease him, or if they were, it was Rosier who had his attention elsewhere. Though his skull was heavier, he felt lighter. His twists and his sways were so easy that he might've believed he was flying again. Meanwhile, Asmodeus struggled at his side, following Rosier's lead and stumbling at times but always quick to regain balance. Rosier laughed brightly when both of them nearly toppled over. He found that he was smiling so much that he could hardly see. And he was happy; his heart was swollen with a giggling sort of delight.

It's the heart that can make us a paradise, even out of hell.

CHAPTER 12

Some millenniums passed, then the devil realized how fruitful the world had become, how abundant in life from the trees, the soil, and creatures that'd begun to tower like in the days before Heaven's war. This was victory; this was evidence that they, fallen and damned things, could create beauty in the absence of God, could build a paradise and even rule themselves. The Lord's adversary ought to have nothing but pride, and it was so: Satan carried not an ounce of shame for the ruin he'd left of Heaven, nor the prince of paradise's weeping during the war, nor for what he had done and would continue to do with his body. He was beauty itself, and he was like God, greater than God. Satan had worked for all of this, he deserved it in a way that his Father never would, and his Father must curse that He cast down His greatest creation, who did no more than create love. Jealousy, jealousy. God was jealous of His perfect devil.

It was as Satan was picking some apples, dropping them into a basket as if he were still full of youthful shame and idiotic timidity, that another revelation bestowed itself upon him. From his arm, the handle of the tightly-woven cradle slid down before tumbling to the grass, each hearty red gift inside it tumbling in a sprawl as if blood. Blood of trees, blood of the Earth. Satan, suddenly, staggered away from it, saw his own shadow inter-mingle with the many apples. His bare feet brushed a stray flower. Scorching, the sun blazed high in the heavens behind him, out of reach and yet here, here. Here, with him. Almost speaking to him.

The fruits. The flowers. The Earth and all her animals.

This was not paradise unheard of; this was not a home that had no ancestor. Satan fell — onto his knees, his hands going over the dirt, feeling the soil that would remain on his palms until he washed them to restore their purity. There had been a time that he'd dabbed his feet clean from the ground of Eden, a time he'd spoken with God, his ankles brushed by the petals of a flowerbed. Once, he had washed God's feet, face bowed submissively. God's hand, one day, had taken Lucifer's jaw, pressed a thumb on his lips, made those golden eyes wondrously peer up at the Creator of all things. The Lord had said that Eden would fall to the Earth; here it was now.

Screaming and howling, the sound of all the fruits and the animals rushed the devil from every direction, and he raised his hands and fisted them into the hair his glorious Father had woven for him. The loving God whose hand was inside him, strumming the chords of the instrument that Lucifer had always been. And the devil laughed and laughed. He doubled over and laughed so hard that it hurt.

Here is free will. Here it is in its truth. Satan, the rebel, always doing what God wanted in the end.

THE NINTH MEMORY

A fter the first few times that Rosier had woken up in Asmodeus' home, he decided to show his friend exactly where he used to sleep — the specific orchards and the specific trunk that he once adored to rest his head upon. He took the older angel's hand and dragged him through a path, saying, "It makes the largest oranges out of all the trees in Heaven. You'll have to help me carry them. You wouldn't mind, would you?"

"Not at all, but you're always ordering me around, Rosier." Asmodeus was craning his head in every direction as he was tugged along, examining every tree like he'd never seen them in his eternal life.

Rosier hummed, then mumbled, "Well, you can go home if you don't want to help, brother."

"I said that I wouldn't mind," Asmodeus chuckled. "You're rather sensitive today, my friend. Is something bothering you?"

Rosier opened his mouth, shut it, then allowed his hand to slip away as a certain massive tree, in between a dozen of a similar size, came into his field of vision. "Oh, look, look!" Hurrying, he left Asmodeus behind and fluttered his wings to propel him forward a little faster. The hanging orange bulbs were even greater than usual, so much that two angel hands wouldn't be enough for a sturdy hold of their bodies. "They're enormous!" Instead of flying, he got on the tips of his toes to reach one of the citrus fruits as he approached; without even having to grab it, the tree promptly let the orange fall onto his palm. But it was so heavy that Rosier's hand dipped beneath it, and he quickly tried to grasp the fruit with both as he staggered in place. Even still, he had to hold it against his body to keep from collapsing with it.

"Lord," Asmodeus said confusedly, but then laughingly. He jogged over to him, took Rosier's hands and helped him with the giant orange. "What's the purpose of a fruit this big at all? Tell the tree to make them smaller."

Rosier huffed up at him. "They're for sharing. It's the perfect size for two angels, maybe three. Once we bring it home, you'll see." A fondness twirled the older angel's lips, his eyes squinted. "Hmm, what are you smiling about?"

"I can't smile?"

"You have a way of smiling that's very..."

"Very?"

"Oh, just tell me what you're smiling about," Rosier sighed, but that only had Asmodeus grin grow wider.

"I just like it when you say that we're going home," was the answer, horribly kind. "I've never had someone live with me, at least not with the intention for them to stay for a long time. It's so new to me, but I like it."

Rosier stared at him, their fingers partly interlocked because of their mutual hold on the orange. "I... like it too." His face flushed pink over his warm brown skin, and Rosier lowered his gaze to their hands. "You're very sweet, Asmodeus. I'm sorry if I shy away from affection. You are so sincere at times that I become embarrassed." A second, then two, of hesitation. "Once we're home, let me cut this orange for you."

"No. I'll do it."

Rosier, adamant, shook his head. "You've given me a nice bed in a nice house. How else am I supposed to thank you? This is where I used to sleep, Asmodeus. I never thought I'd find a resting place more comfortable than here, but I suppose I have now. It makes me very happy. Take it as, well, a sign of love."

"Love?" Angel Asmodeus' eyes softened, surprised and happy. "You love me?"

Rosier scrunched his face, then lifted it to look at his friend. "Of course I do. All angels should love each other. Do you disagree?"

"I don't. I suppose I love you, as well."

"Good," said Rosier. "Let's be sure to never forget it."

Asmodeus nodded. "I know that I won't." He patted the orange, tapping Rosier's fingers. "I'm excited to eat this. Thank you. I love you."

Rosier's face warmed again, but he suppressed a flustered groan and tried walking, urging Asmodeus to follow along. "Yes, yes." Despite his shame, he was delighted to say: "I love you too. I'll love you forever."

ABOUT THE AUTHOR

rafael nicolás is an author of queer fiction. He likes marigolds.

Standing Figure of a Youth,
Giovanni Battista Tiepolo